Rolling with the Punches

Soon, the air was filled with ladies' screams, curses from the men, chairs, bottles and just about anything else that could be picked up and tossed.

Clint reared back his arm to take a heartier swing at the big man and was caught by a surprisingly quick punch to the stomach. Even as he doubled over, he knew he was in trouble. There wasn't anything he could do to prevent what was coming, however, and he was forced to take the big man's knee to his jaw.

Pain lanced through Clint's head, but he was quick enough to turn away at the last moment. Although that kept his jaw from getting busted, it didn't make it hurt any less. The big man's knee slammed into Clint's face like a tree trunk. For a moment, all Clint could see was some sparkling bits of light through a black fog . . .

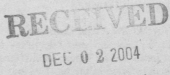

DON'T MISS THESE
ALL-ACTION WESTERN SERIES
FROM THE BERKLEY PUBLISHING GROUP

THE GUNSMITH by J. R. Roberts
Clint Adams was a legend among lawmen, outlaws, and ladies.
They called him . . . the Gunsmith.

LONGARM by Tabor Evans
The popular long-running series about Deputy U.S. Marshal
Long—his life, his loves, his fight for justice.

SLOCUM by Jake Logan
Today's longest-running action Western. John Slocum rides
a deadly trail of hot blood and cold steel.

BUSHWHACKERS by B. J. Lanagan
An action-packed series by the creators of Longarm! The
rousing adventures of the most brutal gang of cutthroats ever
assembled—Quantrill's Raiders.

DIAMONDBACK by Guy Brewer
Dex Yancey is Diamondback, a Southern gentleman turned
con man when his brother cheats him out of the family fortune. Ladies love him. Gamblers hate him. But nobody pulls
one over on Dex . . .

WILDGUN by Jack Hanson
The blazing adventures of mountain man Will Barlow—from
the creators of Longarm!

TEXAS TRACKER by Tom Calhoun
Meet J. T. Law: the most relentless—and dangerous—man-
hunter in all Texas. Where sheriffs and posses fail, he's the
best man to bring in the most vicious outlaws—for a price.

THE GUNSMITH

275

THE LUCKY LADY

J. R. ROBERTS

JOVE BOOKS, NEW YORK

THE BERKLEY PUBLISHING GROUP
Published by the Penguin Group
Penguin Group (USA) Inc.
375 Hudson Street, New York, New York 10014, USA
Penguin Group (Canada), 10 Alcorn Avenue, Toronto, Ontario M4V 3B2, Canada
(a division of Pearson Penguin Canada Inc.)
Penguin Books Ltd., 80 Strand, London WC2R 0RL, England
Penguin Group Ireland, 25 St. Stephen's Green, Dublin 2, Ireland (a division of Penguin Books Ltd.)
Penguin Group (Australia), 250 Camberwell Road, Camberwell, Victoria 3124, Australia
(a division of Pearson Australia Group Pty. Ltd.)
Penguin Books India Pvt. Ltd., 11 Community Centre, Panchsheel Park, New Delhi—110 017, India
Penguin Group (NZ), Cnr. Airborne and Rosedale Roads, Albany, Auckland 1310, New Zealand
(a division of Pearson New Zealand Ltd.)
Penguin Books (South Africa) (Pty.) Ltd., 24 Sturdee Avenue, Rosebank, Johannesburg 2196, South
Africa

Penguin Books Ltd., Registered Offices: 80 Strand, London WC2R 0RL, England

This is a work of fiction. Names, characters, places, and incidents either are the product of the author's imagination or are used fictitiously, and any resemblance to actual persons, living or dead, business establishments, events, or locales is entirely coincidental.

THE LUCKY LADY

A Jove Book / published by arrangement with the author

PRINTING HISTORY
Jove edition / November 2004

Copyright © 2004 by Robert J. Randisi.

ISBN: 0-515-13854-1

JOVE®
Jove Books are published by The Berkley Publishing Group,
a division of Penguin Group (USA) Inc.
375 Hudson Street, New York, New York 10014.
JOVE is a registered trademark of Penguin Group (USA) Inc.
The "J" design is a trademark belonging to Penguin Group (USA) Inc.

PRINTED IN THE UNITED STATES OF AMERICA

10 9 8 7 6 5 4 3 2 1

ONE

It was just another night in The Lucky Lady Saloon.

A warm breeze drifted through the doors, which were always kept propped open after four in the afternoon. That was due to all the foot traffic that came through the place, wearing the carpet that had been thrown down by its owner right to the bare threads.

Red Parks had owned the place from the beginning and had done his best to make The Lucky Lady live up to her name. He'd been lucky to get in on the prosperous establishment, so he meant to dress the saloon up the way every lady should. He'd put carpets onto the floor and spent no small amount of money on the paintings adorning the walls. Red had even commissioned the grandest painting in the place, which hung behind the bar.

That painting was of a nude woman reclining on a bed covered with satin sheets. Her long blond hair flowed over both shoulders, with just the right amount of strands to cover the nipples upon her large breasts. Every inch of skin was smooth as silk and her piercing eyes seemed to hold on every single customer that walked through the door. Red admired that painting and never missed a chance to tell someone how expensive it was.

1

He was also proud of the stage shows that kept the place jumping every night of the week except for Sunday. He had a small pit built next to his stage which was filled with the finest musicians in town. The stage itself was always filled as well, but it was more of a showcase for some of the prettiest faces in town.

All in all, he thought he'd done a damn fine job in whipping that saloon into shape. The Lucky Lady was lucky to have found him, but that didn't explain why Red Parks himself felt so damn unlucky.

Even as he watched people flow through his door, Red scowled and winced at the familiar faces. Of course, they scowled right back at him. It was a collection of dregs and low-lives in a place built for kings. Rather than stand tall as the proud owner of his fine establishment, Red felt more like the tailor who'd put the proverbial dress on a pig.

It hadn't always been like that.

Red told himself that same thing every day and every night. It hadn't always been that way and if he had his say in the matter, it wouldn't be that way for very much longer. No matter how high his hopes were or how noble his intentions, Red still had to deal with things as they stood that night. So far, things didn't look too good.

"Howdy Red," one of the regulars shouted as he stomped into the Lady and wiped his feet on what had once been a fine carpet.

Red tossed his hand up and shook it about while plastering half a smile onto his face. "Hello, Wade."

Wade looked to be in his fifties, but that was only because of his head of thick graying hair. A scraggly beard covered his face as well, hanging down far enough to touch his chest. He was a lean figure, but carried himself with a definite strength.

It was a sight that any saloon owner should have loved to see. The Lucky Lady was packed full and noisy with the sound of dozens of people shouting, drinking and otherwise just carrying on. But Red wasn't happy to see so much commotion, especially when that commotion was too close to where Wade was standing.

Beer sloshed from the mug of a man standing near the front door and sprayed through the air when another man knocked into him. Like plenty of drunks, the man with the beer became instantly fired up and cocked his hand back to take a swing at whoever had bumped him. That motion, in turn, sent even more beer flying through the air.

"Son of a bitch!" Wade shouted as a good deal of that spray landed on the front of his shirt.

The man holding the mostly empty mug shoved the guy in front of him and turned back to his drink. Before he could see how much of his beer he'd spilled, he felt a strong hand clamp down on his shoulder and spin him completely around. When he got his bearings enough to focus his eyes, the man with the mug in his hand found himself staring directly into the weather-worn face of Wade himself.

"That was just rude," Wade said in a voice that was made up of a generous portion of a snarl. "And I hate rudeness in people." With that, Wade cocked his arm back and snapped it forward to drive his fist straight into the other man's face.

The punch landed dead-center, breaking the other man's nose with a wet crunch and splitting his lip in the same blow. Staggering back, the other man dropped his mug so he could press both palms against his face to staunch the flow of blood. Crimson streamed between his fingers and collected in the back of his throat.

Red threw up his hands and tried to rush between Wade and the other man. "Now just hold on a minute here!" he shouted.

But it was too late.

Wade had already moved on to the other men who'd been drinking with the first one and those men, in turn, were doing their best to defend themselves. Not without his own group of friends, Wade plowed straight into the group until reinforcements arrived from his own side.

Chairs scraped against the floor as people either got up from them to join the brawl or pick them up to toss them across the room. Bottles and glasses were already smashing apart either on the edges of furniture or against unwary heads.

Throughout it all, the piano player kept playing. In fact, the entire little orchestra Red had hired only put some more effort into their instruments to raise the overall volume. The musicians were used to fights such as this one and had standing orders to launch into a number whenever a fight began.

Music was supposed to soothe the savage beast, but it didn't seem to be doing too great of a job at the moment. Instead, it simply added to the chaos that filled the saloon and quickly spread to every last corner of The Lucky Lady.

Knowing better than to try to break up the fight at this point, Red covered his face with both hands and did his best to keep low while punches, kicks and every other kind of thing was being thrown around him. From his huddled position, Red couldn't help but focus on one thing in particular as he shuffled toward the relative safety of the bar: his carpet.

That carpet had cost a fortune. That carpet had come from overseas and had been one of the first things he'd bought to dress up his Lucky Lady. Now, like so much else in his place, that carpet was covered with spilled liquor, blood, teeth and shards of glass. Fists grazed off his shoulders and arms as Red continued along his course. The pain he felt was nothing compared to the stabbing in his gut when he saw what had become of his dream.

This wasn't how things were supposed to go. With a place as nice and prosperous as The Lucky Lady, Red was supposed to be a rich man with a beautiful woman at his side. Instead, he was dodging blows in the zoo that his saloon had become. The bar was in his sights. If he could just make it behind the thick wooden barrier, he could at least ride out this storm in relative safety. He could also get to the shotguns stored there for just such an occasion.

Red quickened his pace and reached out with both hands so he could vault himself over the bar. Sure enough, as soon as his guard was lowered, he felt something thump against his head and land directly in front of him.

It was one of the glass ashtrays he'd bought from San Francisco. It had taken him an hour to pick out that particular pattern and now the lovely piece was chipped after knocking against his skull.

Red's vision started to blur and he felt himself passing out.

Just another night at The Lucky Lady Saloon.

TWO

In general, Clint had nothing against the winter. Those were the months that made him feel more alive and made him appreciate little things like a warm fire and something hot to drink. On the other hand, they were also the times when he didn't feel other things like his fingers and toes, for example.

The wind had been getting colder and the nights had taken on a bitter chill as every day went by. When he'd set out last, Clint pointed the nose of his Darley Arabian stallion, Eclipse, toward the west. The mountains had passed from his view as the breezes became less frosty against his cheeks.

Soon, Clint was someplace that didn't get hit too hard at all come wintertime. It was a place that plenty of others had sought out for reasons much grander than a change of scenery or a rise in temperature. Clint had crossed over into California. It wasn't the first time he'd been there, and the country was every bit as beautiful as it had been when he'd last seen it.

While he hadn't escaped the winter's chill completely, Clint found it much easier to bear when he was so close to the scenery surrounding the western coastline. The Pacific wasn't too far away and he even considered riding until he hit water. But rather than push himself too far, Clint decided to stop in the next town for a drink so he could rest up and make his way a little further come sunup.

Eclipse was happy for the break and Clint was happy for a chance to stretch his legs as he walked down the street after putting the stallion up in a stall for the night. Just being in California, the air itself seemed to taste better when he pulled it in through his nose. It filled his lungs and sent a welcome rush through his body.

Anyone who said they didn't understand what made California so special simply hadn't been there. Every time he made it to that part of the country, Clint got an even clearer picture as to what could have pulled so many across the country in their boats, wagons or trains.

Clint had had luck in California before. He'd even considered becoming part owner in a casino or two, but had been lulled away by the promise of the open trail. For the moment, however, the promises held in the California breeze were enough to hold him over.

After a quiet night and a hearty meal, Clint woke up the next morning to feel the first rays of light upon his face. He couldn't help but feel energized, as if the land itself was spurring him onward. Eclipse felt it as well, but then again, the stallion was always ready to run.

By the time San Francisco came into view, Clint thought he and the Darley Arabian could ride all the way across the ocean. Eclipse had worked up enough steam behind his stride that his breath came in powerful bursts while his powerful legs carried them both forward like a runaway train.

Clint almost hated to pull back on the reins, but it was either that or plow straight through the city. Having visited the city plenty of times throughout his travels, Clint knew right where to take Eclipse. The livery workers recognized the Darley Arabian before they set their sights on the man riding him.

"Well, well," the liveryman said. "If it ain't Eclipse himself coming back to pay us a visit."

The worker patted Eclipse's nose and rubbed his neck before finally glancing over at Clint. "Didn't know you'd be in the area, Mister Adams."

"I like to stop in whenever I can," Clint replied. "Hope you've got a stall for me."

"Maybe not for you, but there's always a place for Eclipse, here. I still can't believe Mister Barnum parted with this here beauty."

"It wasn't easy," Clint said, thinking back to the series of events that led the great showman himself to hand over Eclipse's reins. "But it was worth it."

The liveryman had taken up Eclipse's reins and was leading him toward an empty stall. "Indeed, indeed. How long you planning on staying?"

Clint stretched his back and replied, "Don't know yet. I haven't really thought too much about it. I guess long enough to take in the sights and maybe catch up with some old friends."

"Well, Eclipse'll have a spot here for as long as you need it."

"I appreciate that."

"Don't mention it. A man in my line of work appreciates having a fine Darley Arabian like this one around. It boosts the business."

Clint was certain that he'd hear all about that business if he stayed. Although the liveryman was friendly enough, Clint didn't exactly want to hear all the ins and outs of the trade. "I'll be back to check in on him later," he said.

Having ridden into the stable through the wider door in the back, Clint walked out through the front which opened onto the busier section of the street. It was like stepping into a whole other world entirely. Instead of the wide-open spaces of the trail and outskirts of town, he found himself stepping onto a busy street in one of the finest cities in the world.

San Francisco felt like a living thing around him. Its streets were crawling with people and the air was alive with sounds of every sort. There were conversations going on in English, Spanish, Chinese and several other languages depending on which way Clint happened to be facing. Even the smells seemed more exotic as fine cuisine and exotic spices mingled with the salty air blowing in from the ocean.

Clint hadn't taken more than three or four steps before he was planning where he wanted to go next. There were hotels to visit, restaurants to sample and card games to play. Although a poker game was never too hard to find throughout the country, it had been a while since Clint had partaken in some high-stakes gambling.

There was a different mindset that came when the stakes were raised. It kept a man's edge sharp the way only risking it all ever could. And even if he didn't settle on a particular place or game for the evening, Clint knew something interesting would surely find him. San Francisco was just like that.

If only he knew how right he was.

THREE

The Lighthouse Inn hadn't been on Clint's short list of places to visit while in San Francisco. In fact, the place hadn't been on his list at all. The only reason he was there was because it had been built on the site of one of his favorite restaurants and was also big enough to see from a mile away.

It was one of those places that was so new, it still smelled like freshly sawed timber. More than that, however, The Lighthouse appeared to be a fine place in its own regard. There were two floors to the building, which took up nearly a quarter of a block on its own. Facing out toward the water, there was a beautiful view out half of the windows and Clint was enjoying that view moments after walking in.

Instead of the tinny piano that was the bulk of most smaller saloons' entertainment, The Lighthouse boasted an entire string quartet. The music gave the place a sense of real elegance. Of course, the generally formal dress of its patrons didn't hurt matters either. Clint was still admiring a woman in a fancy dress with a plunging neckline when he was approached by a slender fellow decked out in a tuxedo.

"Is there anything I can do for you?" the man asked, not even trying to hide the distaste in his voice.

Clint could feel the other man's gaze lingering on his clothes which were still covered with generous helpings of trail dust. "Do you have any rooms to rent?"

The man in the tuxedo cocked his eyebrows as though he was trying desperately not to laugh at Clint's question. "Yes, but they are quite expensive. This is one of the city's finest hotels."

Clint's eyes drifted over to the card tables, which were set up in a room just off of the main lobby. He was an experienced enough player to be able to spot his most likely targets without much trouble. In seconds, he'd picked out the exact spot where he wanted to sit.

"Tell you what," Clint said, "I'll make you a deal."

"Excuse me?"

"You work in a fine establishment like this. I'm sure you're familiar with the gamblers' circuit."

"I am."

"Then I'm sure you play the occasional hand or at least try your luck every so often." Clint could tell he was chipping through the other man's frosty exterior, but he still felt like having a little fun with him.

Sure enough, the man in the tuxedo glanced in the direction Clint was looking. When he looked back, he already seemed just a little bit friendlier. "I've been known to bet on occasion."

"Then I've got a bet for you," Clint said, producing a silver dollar from his pocket. "Put me down for a room. If I can take this dollar over to that casino and win fifty more in an hour or less, you need to put me up in a suite for the price of my opening bet."

"A suite for a dollar?"

"Not only that, but a suite for my entire stay here for a dollar."

"That's a different story."

Clint held the dollar out enticingly.

"And what if you can't win that much in an hour?" the well-dressed man asked.

"Ah, now there's the good part. If I can't make good on my bet, I'll take the smallest room you've got for one night and I'll pay you enough for that suite for the entire week."

The other man's eyebrows perked up at that prospect and he took one more look at the casino. After studying Clint a bit longer, he finally nodded and said, "All right. You've got yourself a bet. But I should warn you that we hold men to their word here at The Lighthouse."

"A man should be held to his word no matter where he is," Clint responded.

"True enough. I'll keep my eye on you." And without another word, the man in the tuxedo plucked a watch from his vest pocket and flipped it open. "Whenever you're ready."

"Take these up to my room, if you please," Clint said, handing over his saddlebags to the less-than-receptive host.

Despite the awkward load he was carrying, the man in the tux still maintained his dignity. Underneath it all, there was something else keeping his spirits up: the smugness of a man who knew he'd just put money down on a sure thing. Keeping that in mind was more than enough to make him happy even as he lugged a dusty set of worn saddlebags behind the front desk.

Clint flipped the coin into the air and caught it with a quick flick of his wrist. From there, he stuck it into his pocket so he could rub his hands together while heading into the casino.

"I'm not real good at this game," Clint said as he crossed the room and approached the table he'd selected. "But I sure would like to play. Can we keep the stakes low to start off?"

Furtive glances were exchanged around the table until one of the players gave Clint a smile that reminded him of a shark opening its jaws to a guppy. "Take a seat," the gambler said. "We'll take it easy on ya."

Forty-five minutes later, Clint was being shown into his suite by the man in the tuxedo as well as a kid dressed in a smart-looking red outfit. The kid carried the saddlebags this time as the man in the tuxedo held the door open for Clint.

"Now this is what I call a room!" Clint said as he stepped into the suite, which was easily triple the size of a normal hotel room.

"This is our finest suite." Rolling his eyes, the host added, "It was the only one still available."

"Don't feel too bad . . ." Clint paused before asking, "What's your name?"

"Bert."

"Don't feel too bad about it, Bert. A sporting man like you deserves a second chance. How about a game tonight? I'll buy the drinks?"

For the first time since Clint had arrived, enough of the host's facade melted away for him to look like just another guy dressed up in a fancy suit. "I think I'll take you up on that," Bert said. "By the way, what name should I put on the register?"

"Clint Adams. And here," he added, peeling off a few layers from his winnings to add to Bert's tip, "buy some drinks for my friends at the card table. I don't think they know what hit 'em."

FOUR

After Clint had gotten himself rested up and settled in his room, he was ready to head back downstairs to take advantage of what the new hotel had to offer. His suite was actually big enough for him to settle in even if he'd been carrying all of his earthly possessions along with him. The suite was bigger than some houses he'd seen and stretched out through three different rooms.

Once Bert shut the door and left him alone in his room, Clint walked around and started to feel bad about taking up so much space. That feeling vanished the instant he got a look at his bed. With several weeks of sleeping on cots or even the ground behind him, Clint was nearly knocked off his feet by the sight of the huge, inviting mattress.

It was big enough for Eclipse to stretch out on and the moment Clint's back hit it, the mattress comforted him like a loving hand. Despite the fact that he was excited to be in town and start in on his exploring, Clint damn near fell asleep right then and there. He meant to fight the nap that he felt creeping up on him, but then gave in, stretched out, and rested his hat over his eyes.

He only dozed for an hour or so and when he awoke,

he was even more raring to go. One quick request was all it took to have hot water brought up to fill the bathtub in his room. Clint wasn't sure if Bert was being friendly or insulting when he made sure to include scented salts and powders along with the water. Either way, Clint soon realized he needed the extra help and indulged while washing away the grit and dust that had collected on him after so long on the trail.

Although he wasn't in the habit of dressing like a dandy for supper, Clint dug down into the bottom of his bags where he kept the garments reserved for special occasions. The clothes were still neatly folded and clean, mainly because they hadn't been out of that bag for so long.

Still outclassed by Bert's attire, Clint checked himself over in a full-length mirror in the separate dressing room just off of the bedroom. The starched white shirt still fit him perfectly, as did the light gray suit waistcoat. He couldn't remember the last time he'd had any reason to dress so formally, but this seemed like as good a time as any.

Stepping out of his suite, Clint couldn't help but feel like some rich businessman or socialite. Folks tended to look at a man differently when he was dressed up, as opposed to looking like a cowboy with a gun strapped around his waist. Of course, Clint was still wearing his gun belt, but it was concealed beneath the waistcoat which had been specially tailored to do just that. The modified Colt hung at Clint's side, its weight feeling as much a part of him as his arms hanging from his shoulders.

"Hello there, Mister Adams," an unfamiliar man said as Clint came walking through the lobby. "I trust your room is satisfactory?"

Clint stopped and studied the other man, who appeared to be at least ten years older than Bert but dressed in a similar tuxedo. When he was certain the other man wasn't kidding, Clint replied, "Is there anyone on earth who wouldn't find that room satisfactory?"

"You'd be surprised. I'm Karl Patrice, the owner of The Lighthouse."

"Glad to meet you, Karl. I've got to hand it to you, this is one hell of a place you've got here."

"Thank you very much. That means a lot coming from a man like yourself, Mister Adams."

"Please, just call me Clint."

"All right then," Karl said, taking a moment as though using someone's first name required an actual adjustment within his own head. "Clint."

Giving Karl a light slap on the shoulder, Clint said, "That didn't hurt now, did it?"

Just like Bert before him, Karl was starting to lighten up after just a few moments of being talked to like he wasn't some caretaker dressed in a fancy suit. "Not at all."

"By the way, even though the room is great, I'll be happy to move into something smaller. I kind of got my way in there by having a bit of fun with Bert a little earlier. If that caused any problems, I'm sure any room I can get will be just fine."

"Oh, don't worry about it." Karl winced when he added, "I'll admit that I didn't exactly like the way things turned out since that is one of our most expensive suites, but there's no problem at all. Once I saw whose name was on the register, I figured we'd more than make up for a loss like that. In fact, if I'd known you were coming, I would have insisted you stay in that very room anyway."

"Really?"

"Sure. I think that having a man like you here will draw some business my way. I'm sure you understand."

Clint laughed a bit and shrugged. "I never really thought of it like that, but if that's all you need to get a boost, then I'm willing. I hope you don't think I'm going to start any trouble just to make headlines, because I'm not about to—"

"Oh no," Karl interrupted. "Nothing like that! I meant your reputation at the card tables. I used to travel the gamblers' circuit myself and you've got quite an impressive list of credits among that group. Why, Bat Masterson himself had nothing but kind words to say about you."

"How's Bat doing?"

"Fine, fine. He's kept busy out East and is doing quite well for himself. Your name's even come up in conversation at a game I had with Doc Holliday, but that was a few years ago."

"It's been some time since I saw Doc and he didn't look so good."

"Doc never really looked too good, but he kept on going."

"You know something? I'll bet you're absolutely right about that."

Noticing some new arrivals walking through the front doors, Karl took a breath and straightened the collar of his shirt. With those few simple actions, he seemed to turn back into the picture of a proper gentleman. His voice even seemed overly formal as he turned back to Clint wearing his professional expression once more.

"Anyway," Karl said. "Welcome to San Francisco, Mister Adams. Sorry. Make that Clint. And enjoy your stay here at The Lighthouse. If you need anything at all, please just let me know."

"I'll be sure to do that."

"Now, if you'll excuse me, I've got some other guests to see to." And with that, Karl walked away and made a straight line for the new arrivals. By Clint's standards, the two finely dressed couples that had entered the lobby appeared to be well-to-do. Karl probably saw them as a payday on eight legs.

Clint couldn't help but feel his spirits brighten after

having talked to Karl. Although he certainly appreciated getting the royal treatment, he couldn't help but wonder what the hell Bat and Doc had said about him to warrant such high marks. Bat was a good friend and Doc had his moments, but neither one of them were exactly the types to talk someone up that much while playing cards.

Then again, there was always the possibility that Karl had been a bigger presence on the circuit than he'd let on. Saloon and casino owners liked to cater to the big gamblers, but a serious professional gambler would have the nose to sniff out any and all of the players worth catering to.

Rather than try to figure everything out, Clint decided to sit back and enjoy the perks of being recognized. Lord knows, there were plenty of drawbacks that went along with it. At least this time the man who'd recognized him wasn't taking a shot at him.

FIVE

"So what have you heard?" Red asked, the moment he saw who'd just come walking through the door to his office.

The man who entered the quiet room in the back of The Lucky Lady was average height with a round build. A good-sized belly hung over his belt and his face was covered with a well-groomed beard. The top of his head wasn't quite so covered, as the hair up there had thinned out over the last few of his forty-one years.

Walking all the way into the office, the man pulled the door shut behind him. He didn't seem too anxious to respond to the question that had been posed to him by the saloon's owner.

"Well?" Red insisted. "If you're not going to say anything, you might as well go right back out that door."

"He's in San Francisco."

Red placed both hands flat upon his desk. "Are you sure about that, Bo? Right now, I don't need to be messing about with any more rumors."

Bo Walsh had been working for Red since before The Lucky Lady had opened. He was one of the few people on Red's payroll who could speak his mind without too much worry and he was also one of the few men who Red truly cared to hear from.

"It's not a rumor," Bo said. "I heard from a friend of mine that he's there. I checked in with some other fellows I know there and they confirmed it."

Red practically jumped up from his chair. "Do you know how long he'll be staying in San Francisco?"

"Long enough for me to get there and have a word with him," Bo replied, answering Red's next question before it even had to be asked.

"Excellent. When do you leave?"

After taking a moment to think, Bo said, "If I leave tonight, I should make it to The Lighthouse either tomorrow night or the next afternoon." Inside, Bo winced. He'd made a slip-up in that last sentence, which he hoped Red didn't catch.

Judging by the scowl that had suddenly appeared on Red's face, he'd caught it just fine.

"Did you say The Lighthouse?" Red asked.

Trying not to react in a way that would make things worse, Bo simply said, "Yeah."

The anger was like a little squall that boiled up quickly into a full-fledged storm. "He's staying at The Lighthouse?"

"Yeah, Red. That's what I heard."

"Karl Patrice's Lighthouse?"

"That would be the place."

"Aw, Jesus." Red slumped back down into his chair as though he'd been dropped into it. "We'll have a hell of a time getting him away from that place. If I know Karl, he'll be giving Adams the royal treatment just to keep him there."

Bo's brow furrowed. "Why would he do that?"

"Ah, you don't know about this business. Keeping a known man in your place draws in the kind of people who make saloon owners rich. Plus, it's good for security.

Keeps the riffraff away when they know someone like The Gunsmith is playing cards there."

"I heard The Lighthouse isn't just a saloon, Red."

"I know that! It was just a word."

"So do you still want me to go to San Francisco?"

After pulling in a deep breath and letting it out with a controlled sigh, Red nodded. "Go ahead and go. And take this with you." Opening a drawer in his desk, Red pulled out a bundle tied together with twine and sealed for good measure. "It's my offer to Adams."

"What if it's not good enough?"

"Then take matters into your own hands. Do anything you need to get the job done and I don't give a damn how messy things need to get."

"Are you sure about that?"

"Take a look around," Red said. "Take a good, long look."

Bo turned to look where Red was pointing, which was through a narrow, rectangular window looking out onto the main room of the saloon. "I see what you mean."

"Yeah, and I've been looking at that for way too long. So you get Clint Adams to take that offer or don't even bother coming back."

"What about someone else? Isn't there anyone who could—"

"It's Adams or nobody," Red cut in. "Now go."

Knowing better than to argue with his boss at that moment, Bo gathered up the things he needed to bring with him and left the office. He took Red completely at his word. If he wasn't able to sway Clint Adams one way or another, he simply would pull up stakes and settle somewhere else. That would sure as hell beat the alternative.

SIX

It hadn't taken Clint too long to get used to receiving the royal treatment. Of course, it hadn't taken him long to see why he was being treated so well either. In the time that he'd been in town, Clint hadn't even entertained the thought of staying anywhere but The Lighthouse. He'd done some wandering throughout San Francisco, but had always come back to his new base of operations.

And in the time that he'd used The Lighthouse as his base of operations, Clint had noticed the business in that particular saloon pick up. In fact, he guessed the amount of people gambling and drinking had at least doubled over the last couple of days.

That was apparently the amount of time needed for word to spread about the new player holding court at a table reserved just for him in The Lighthouse's casino. Not only had several local faces become familiar to Clint as he played hand after hand of poker, but other faces came into the saloon which would have been familiar to any professional gambler. With those familiar faces, the games had become more interesting and the stakes had climbed up through the roof. Along with that came more drinks being bought, more dance hall girls making their rounds and more patronage for The Lighthouse Inn.

Even though the smile on Karl's face was difficult to miss, Clint didn't have much reason to frown, himself. He was staying in a lavish room in one of the finest cities in the country and was taking in a load of winnings at the poker tables. A place like The Lighthouse didn't put up with cheaters, especially since the higher class players didn't mind losing every so often so they could keep taking their stab at the pot.

It was also a kind of vicious cycle because Clint knew well enough that him being in that casino was keeping away a good deal of cheats and sharps. That surely made Karl's smile even wider. A profitable arrangement, to be sure, but at least it was profitable for everyone concerned.

Clint had been in San Francisco just over a week, but the days had started to blend together in a constant flow of music, poker hands and free beers. When he took a moment to think about it, Clint felt like he needed to get outside and breathe some air that didn't carry the taint of cigar smoke. As always, Karl spotted it the moment Clint got up from his chair.

"What's wrong, Clint?" Karl asked. "What can I get for you?"

"Relax, Karl. I just need to get outside for a minute."

"If there's anything you need, all you have to do is ask."

Clint was walking toward the door when he realized Karl was still dogging his every step. Stopping suddenly, Clint thought he might just feel the hotel owner run right into him.

"I've been sitting so much lately that I feel like there's roots connecting me to that chair," Clint said. "You think you can do anything for me about that?"

"Well, I guess I could—"

"Forget I asked," Clint interrupted. "Just tend to the

rest of your customers for a while. I'm starting to feel like an exhibit."

"Pardon me?"

"Actually, there is something you can do for me."

Reacting as though he suddenly began to understand the language Clint was speaking, Karl's entire face lit up. "Anything you need."

"You stand right there," Clint said, pointing to the spot Karl's feet were currently filling. Moving his fingers to point outside, he added, "And I'll stand over there. Sound good?"

The hotel owner nodded and let his shoulders drop from where they'd been bunched up around his ears. "Point taken. If anyone asks, I'll just tell them you'll be back in a while."

Clint patted the other man on the shoulder and headed for the front door. When he stepped outside, he wasn't quite sure what he was going to find. Having spent so much time at the poker table, Clint had lost track of whether the skies had been cloudy or clear, or even if the breeze was cool or warm. Sometimes, he even lost track of the time of day it was. All of that was easy enough to do when his entire world became one hand of poker after another.

That didn't mean that Clint wasn't having the time of his life. On the other hand, there was something about what Karl had said right before Clint had managed to get out of The Lighthouse on his own. That part about Karl fielding questions if anyone else asked where Clint had gone. What bothered Clint wasn't the other man's offer.

It was the fact that Clint knew there would be other people asking about him.

Once he was outside, Clint lifted his eyes to the sky and let the entire city wash over him. There were sights, sound and smells that he took in right there that he couldn't get anywhere outside of San Francisco. A couple more minutes was all he would need to get some wind back into his sails. After that, he might find someplace to eat and then he would be ready for some more poker.

With that thought, Clint was able to put some things into perspective. There were worse situations for him to be in and much worse places to find himself than a pampered gambler in the heart of San Francisco. Sure, Karl was profiting from Clint patronizing The Lighthouse, but Clint was having one hell of a time there.

Maybe it was the breeze coming in off the bay or perhaps it was the dark purple hue of the dusky sky that made his spirits lift even higher. The city itself had its own energy, which got Clint's blood flowing the way logs stoked a fire. The suit he wore was less than two days old and had been tailored just for him, which made him feel even more like he was right where he belonged.

Besides playing one exhilarating game of cards after another, Clint had taken enough of his share of winnings to keep him comfortable for several months on the trail. But there was something else that had lifted Clint's spirits in that last minute or so. All he needed to do to find it was take his eyes from the sky and look at the slender, shapely woman walking straight toward him.

"Looks like it's going to be a lovely night," she said to him.

"Why yes," Clint replied. "It certainly does."

SEVEN

Her hair was light brown with streaks of an almost golden blond mixed throughout. She wore it straight down her back and the natural flow of it gave her thick mane a natural, curly bounce. That wasn't the only part of her with bounce, however, as Clint was quick to see for himself. She had a trim body with curves that were just right for her slender frame.

"My name's Amy," she said, extending a hand.

Taking her hand and squeezing gently, he replied, "Clint Adams."

Her eyes narrowed a bit. "I think I may have heard of you. Aren't you a professional card player?"

"I've been known as worse things, that's for certain."

"Me too." When she said that, Amy added a sly grin that made her seem more attractive all the way around. Of course, that didn't mean that she wasn't already playing with a winning hand.

She wore a red silk dress with a pattern of white flowers that extended down her sides and along the entire length of her skirt. The blouse was tied up the front, exposing the upper curve of her cleavage, which looked inviting and forbidden at the same time. Her hips were

slight, but with just enough of a curve for Clint to imagine
how good it would feel to run his hands down over them.

"Are you new to San Francisco?" Clint asked.

"Actually, yes. I only just arrived."

"It's a fine city."

"It certainly is. As much as I'd like to take in the
sights, my only problem is knowing where to start."

"So you're saying you need a guide?"

She smiled and lowered her eyes. When she looked
back up again, there was a smoldering quality about her
that said she knew what she wanted and was already closing in on it. "A guide would be just what I needed. Especially if he's about six-foot-two with dark hair and
lovely eyes."

"I don't stare into my own eyes too much, but I think
I may just fit the rest of that bill."

"You know something? You may just be exactly who
I was looking for."

Clint felt her arm wrap around his as Amy fell into
step beside him. "Are you here on your own?"

"Not anymore," she replied.

As quickly as the last couple of days had flown by, the
next few hours flew by even faster. Clint still didn't know
much about Amy or why she'd taken such a shine to him,
but that didn't seem to matter. They were both just two
people enjoying the night and since neither of them
seemed to want any more than that, Clint was willing to
let it stay right there.

They walked all the way through town and wound up
at a little restaurant in the Chinese section which served
some of the best fried rice Clint had ever tasted. The place
as well as the company made him feel as though he was
spending time in another part of the world instead of just
a previously unexplored section of San Francisco.

Once they stuck their noses back outside, the darkness
was like a thick velvet curtain which wrapped around

them both. Her grip tightened on his arm and Clint found
the warmth of her body very comforting indeed. All this
time, they hadn't stopped talking. What made the night
fly by even more, however, was the fact that they hadn't
once touched upon a subject more serious than their var-
ied travels or ideas for the next place they should visit.

Finally, she said something that brought Clint's
thoughts all the way back to where they'd started.

"I've heard that you're staying at The Lighthouse,"
Amy said. "Do you think you could show me that place
next?"

"It's fine so long as you enjoy watching poker being
played."

"Don't they have shows and music there as well?"

"Sure, but if I get anywhere near those tables, it won't
be long before I'm roped into a game."

She studied him for a moment and laughed under her
breath. "Something tells me you really wouldn't mind being roped in that direction."

"No," Clint said, leaning in closer to her, "but I can
think of some other places I'd rather go before the night's
out."

"Why, Clint Adams, I'm appalled," Amy said in a tone
of voice that was anything but convincing. "I'm a proper
lady and as such, I'd like to wait until I hear anything
else along such suggestive lines."

"How about after a dance or two and a few hands of
cards?"

Suddenly, her expression went from something close
to insulted to disappointed. "You wanted to wait that
long? I must be doing something wrong."

Amy's entire face lit up when she stepped into The Lighthouse's main parlor. The room was enormous, filled with
the stage, several tables and the spot reserved for the musicians. The casino wasn't too far away and the smells of

dinner still hung in the air like a gourmet breeze.

Even though he'd been living there since his arrival, Clint had to admit the place was pretty impressive. The effect was even greater after dark, when the lights inside didn't have any competition from on high. As if all of that wasn't enough to impress the woman on his arm, Clint was almost instantly spotted by the owner of the establishment and pounced upon like the last scrap of food.

"Good evening, Clint," Kari exclaimed. "I trust your walk was refreshing. It's certainly a good night for it."

As much as Clint hadn't wanted to let any of this go to his head, he couldn't resist the opportunity to play it up a bit. "It certainly was a delightful walk," Clint said in a fancy tone of voice. "Is my regular table ready?"

"Of course."

"Then keep my seat warm. I'll be there as soon as I've shown this fine young lady around."

Karl shot a look over to Amy and was unable to keep the smile on his face. After a curt nod, he turned on his heels and left them alone.

Clint still had his nose in the air when he glanced over to Amy and was unable to keep himself from laughing after she gave him a questioning look. "I know, I know," he said with a shrug. "I can't explain it myself. But if I tell him that a few free beers and a meal or two would be enough to keep me happy, they might just kick me out of my suite."

That made Amy's eyes go wide as saucers. "You've got your own suite?"

"I sure do."

She moved in closer to him until Clint could feel the warmth of her body and could smell the perfumed scent of her hair. When she took a small step forward, Amy was sure to rub her leg against Clint's. It hadn't been the first such temptation she'd offered, but it sure had a good effect upon him.

"I've heard the suites in this city are some of the best in the country," she said in a voice that was just slightly louder than a whisper. "Do you think I could see yours?"

Clint leaned down until his face was almost close enough to place a kiss upon her lips. He stopped just short and replied, "All you had to do was ask."

EIGHT

Bo Walsh had only just arrived in San Francisco, but he still felt as though he was in the seat he'd occupied on the train. After being pulled over those rails, he could still feel the jostling in his bones and his blood still felt as if it was rattling within his veins. Normally, he didn't mind taking a train. This time, however, there was too much else going on for him to enjoy the trip.

This time was strictly about business and nothing else.

He knew damn well that if he didn't complete the task he'd been given, he might as well just lay his head on the same rails that had brought him to town and wait for the next train to finish him off. The iron wheels of any locomotive would certainly be more forgiving than Red.

Bo checked the two most important things he'd brought with him for the task at hand. For about the thousandth time, he patted the inner pocket of his jacket where he kept the bundle Red had given him. He then checked to make sure that the .32 caliber pistol was still in the holster under his opposite shoulder. Even though he knew he'd be needing one more than the other, it was comforting to know that both of those things were there.

It hadn't been too long ago since the last time he'd

been in San Francisco and the streets hadn't changed one bit. Bo walked the way he needed to go without once looking around to take in the sights. He knew how breathtaking the city could be. At least, he thought that way on just about any of his other visits but this time was different.

This time, he had a job to do and a messy one at that. No matter how sticky things might get, he had to do that job all the same. It was either that, or catch a train to anywhere else but back home because there wouldn't be much of anything waiting for him there anyhow if he failed.

Bo cleared his throat and ran his fingers through his hair as he walked. It felt better to get some fresh air since he'd been telling himself that same line of nonsense ever since he left Red's office. Well, there might have been some parts that were more nonsense than others, but enough of it was true to keep the knot tied tightly in his stomach.

Like most things that worried a man, the longer he thought about them, the worse they got. Bo had been working himself up into a lather the entire time and he knew it. Unfortunately, there wasn't much for him to do about it besides just get to work and get it all over with. To that end, he quickened his steps down the street until he caught his first sight of The Lighthouse Inn.

From the angle of his approach, there wasn't much he could see of The Lighthouse that was too awe-inspiring. In fact, all he could really make out was the angle of its roof. But even from the back and without the benefit of all the fancy signs and fanfare, The Lighthouse was still a sight to behold.

Most of that was because Bo knew about the history of the place and all the competition it had in San Francisco. He'd heard enough of those stories from Red. It wasn't even the first time Bo had been to the place. He'd scouted it out plenty of times when it was being built as well as when it was getting its start soon after opening its doors.

Truth be told, staying at The Lighthouse had been one of the best times he'd ever had. Bo had been treated like a king and even though that was mainly Karl Patrice's way of getting under Red's skin, that time had still been a hoot for Bo Walsh.

This trip, Bo knew, would not be a hoot. In fact, he caught himself coming to a stop as he thought about the past and forced himself to keep walking down the street and around the corner. Finally, the front of The Lighthouse came into view and it was even better than it had been the last time he'd seen it. Business had obviously been good and Karl had made some changes. That only cinched the knot in Bo's gut a little tighter.

Pulling in a deep breath, Bo checked his essentials one more time. The bundle was still there, as was the gun. His hand lingered a bit longer this time upon the grip of the .32. Although the weapon didn't untie the knot in his stomach, it did a good job of allowing Bo to forget the discomfort for a moment. He had a job to do. No matter what else, he couldn't forget about that. There was a job to do and precious little time to do it.

Ignoring the inviting glances from the dancing girls and the soiled doves making their rounds through the crowd, Bo headed straight for the bartender after bolting straight through the lobby. Someone behind the front desk may have said something to him, but Bo wasn't listening. In fact, he barely realized the lobby was even there.

Taken aback for a moment by the intensity in Bo's eyes, the bartender quickly regained his composure and asked, "What can I do for you?"

"Clint Adams," Bo snapped. "I need to see him. Right now."

NINE

There had been plenty of times when Clint had thought about sharing the enormous bed that took up a good portion of his suite's bedroom. But even though there had been plenty of ladies who caught his eye, there simply weren't enough hours in the day to give them time as well as tend to all the other things on his plate.

Clint knew plenty well that a man needed to make time for the finer things in life, but he hadn't been compelled to focus in that direction when there was so much else around. He hadn't been compelled, that is, until he got close to Amy.

She had a way about her that made her stand apart from the others. She looked at him without trying to restrain the desires going through her mind and body. And when she touched him, Clint could feel the woman's passion like a heat boiling just beneath her surface.

All the others were attracted like so many of the customers walking in and out through The Lighthouse's doors. Those ladies had their charms, but they simply wanted to be with him because of who he was. They wanted to tell their friends that they'd been with Clint Adams, The Gunsmith. Or perhaps they wanted a sweet little secret to keep for themselves that they'd shared a bed with a famous gambler and gunslinger.

Most of that could be blamed on Karl and his incessant bragging about who was staying at his inn. But Amy had nothing to do with Karl. She was someone much different from the ladies lounging about the casino looking for some kind of erotic trophy to mount.

Amy may have had some things that she wasn't telling him, but she didn't just want to bed The Gunsmith. She just wanted him.

Clint was a good enough judge of character to know the difference.

Of course, there was something much more basic that drew Clint more toward Amy than to the rest he'd met while on his recent visit to San Francisco. It was something much more primal and it cut a lot deeper than any part of her character.

She wanted him and he wanted her. Sometimes, that was all that mattered.

They stumbled into Clint's suite already entangled in each other's arms. Amy fumbled with the buttons of Clint's shirt in her haste to get him out of his clothes. He, on the other hand, had been anticipating the moment long enough to plan every move his hands would make once they finally got the chance.

The instant Clint's hands slipped through the opening made by a few popped buttons and touched Amy's bare flesh, she pulled in a quick breath and her muscles tensed. She froze in the middle of what she was doing and leaned her head back slightly to savor the feel of his hands delving deeper beneath the material she wore.

Clint was savoring the moment as well. He'd just gotten his hand under her blouse and was about to peel it off of her, but he held off. Instead, he prolonged the moment by massaging her flesh and probing to find the spots that made her start to tremble in his arms.

When her eyes opened, Amy smiled widely at him. That was like the opening of a floodgate and marked the moment when the last shred of their inhibitions was officially cast aside. Their hands moved quickly now until they were both in a frenzy to feel as much naked skin as possible. Their eyes were focused on each other and every one of their motions was directed at either disrobing the other or squirming to allow themselves to be undressed.

Neither of them was even paying attention to where they were moving within the room. In fact, Amy seemed to be caught off her guard when she was forced to come to a stop. Clint had been pulling her along with him as he worked his way across the front room toward the bedroom. With his senses focused elsewhere, however, Clint wound up bumping into a comfortably padded chaise lounge instead of stepping into the next room.

That didn't seem to bother either one of them. In fact, when she noticed where they were standing, Amy pushed Clint back using both hands until she felt him stumble and drop down onto the chaise. Until that moment, Clint had merely considered the chaise to be just an odd, garishly decorated piece of incomplete furniture. It wasn't quite a couch and wasn't quite a bed, so he'd just decided to ignore it.

Now, as he dropped onto the floral print cushions, Clint had no trouble at all finding a perfectly good use for the chaise. Amy practically tore off his jeans and tossed them aside. Clint slid his hand up over her legs until he felt the soft ruffles of her undergarments. When he pulled the delicates off of her, Clint saw Amy's eyes widen and could feel the warm dampness between her thighs.

Clint pulled off his shirt because, at that point, clothes just seemed to be getting in the way. As he reached out to do the same for her, Amy stepped back and gave him a teasing waggle of her finger.

"Ah, ah, ah," she scolded playfully. Stepping back a

foot or two from Clint, Amy seemed to be putting some
distance between herself and the man in front of her.
However, it soon became apparent that she wasn't so
much trying to get away, but just to give Clint a better
view of the show she had planned.

Amy ran her fingers along the front of her blouse
which was hanging open to reveal the corset underneath.
Untying the corset by slowly tugging on the strings that
held it together, she arched her back and made a sound
that reminded Clint of a purr as she removed it and the
blouse altogether. Her breasts were pert and just the right
size, capped with dark brown nipples that were already
erect with anticipation.

Once her top was naked, Amy took a step toward Clint.
She still wouldn't let him touch her just yet and pushed
away his hands when he reached out for her. Clint was
still entranced by her display and felt even more excited
when his advance was denied.

Judging by the smirk on her face, Amy was perfectly
aware of every bit of the effect she was having upon him.
Not only that, but she used his reactions to figure out what
he liked the best so she could do that even more. She saw
Clint's expression when she brushed her fingers across her
own nipples and slowly moved her hands back to that
same spot.

Once there, she indulged herself by touching the sensitive skin of her breasts, pinching her nipples slightly
until she felt the tingle of pleasure rush through her body.
Amy was moving toward Clint again, but it wasn't out of
some plan to entice him. She seemed to just drift toward
him as though her every instinct wanted to get closer.

This time, when she felt his hands upon her, she didn't
push them away. Instead, she clasped her hands on top of
his and guided him to the precise spot that she wanted to
be touched. That perfect openness was undeniably erotic,
making Clint feel as though he was truly experiencing

Amy's body rather than taking what he wanted from her.

Clint felt her hands move off of his, but he wasn't inclined to move his own hands from exactly where they were. Her nipples were poking against his palms and she moaned under her breath as he rubbed his hands back and forth over them.

She was moving closer now, climbing on top of him and pressing Clint down onto the chaise. Her hands were busy moving between his legs so she could stroke his cock which was already rigid and ready for her. Using one hand to steady herself, she got one foot on either side of him so she could squat down on top of him.

The lips of her vagina were hot and wet as Clint's penis glided over them. When she shifted her weight so she could allow him inside of her, Amy let out a slow, steady breath until she rode him all the way down. Clint leaned back, closed his eyes, and savored the moment. Just then, he couldn't help but think about an old expression that fit him like a glove.

It was good to be king.

TEN

Indeed, Clint had never felt so much like royalty until that very instant. The Lighthouse Inn wasn't too far from being a palace and the suite he'd been given was grand in more ways than one. Now, being straddled by a beautiful woman on a piece of furniture fancier than most folks' homes, Clint thought the only thing he was missing was a crown.

That thought flashed through his mind, only to be pushed aside by more important things. Mainly, the touch of Amy's fingers as she traced her nails over his chest, sparking little bursts of pleasure as she went, was more than enough to snap him back into the moment.

Her body was gorgeous writhing on top of him. And there was something achingly sexy about her keeping her skirt on as she moved back and forth with him inside of her. Amy's legs shifted beneath the thin folds of material that Clint hadn't managed to get off of her. The motion of her waist made the fabric rub against him as well, making every little wriggle a welcome surprise.

All this time, Amy was slowly dragging her fingers down his body. She'd lingered for a while here and there, but now she was approaching the part of him that would normally be below the belt. Her hands slipped beneath the fabric of her skirt, which was now twisting around herself and him as well.

She lifted the skirt like she was still a little shy about showing herself. The contrast of that and the way she slowly rode his cock made Clint even harder inside of her. With one hand, she reached down to rub herself as well as Clint's penis as it slid in and out of her. With the other hand, she held the skirt down so he couldn't exactly see what she was doing.

In the end, she got exactly what she'd been after. Clint had restrained himself so he could allow her to pleasure him, but even he was human and wasn't made of stone. Unable and unwilling to hold back any longer, Clint grabbed her around the waist and pumped his hips up to drive up inside of her.

This time, she was the one to be taken to another level of ecstasy as her eyes practically rolled up inside their sockets. Amy's hands reflexively searched out Clint's bare skin and she dropped all pretenses of trying to tease him by covering herself with her skirt. The moment she felt Clint take hold of her and start pounding up into her wet pussy, Amy let out a wanton moan and clenched her eyes shut.

The sight of her on top of him was almost enough to drive Clint straight out of his mind. Not only did her pussy clench tightly around his cock as he thrust it into her, but Amy arched her back in a way that made her breasts stand out in a proud display. Clint held onto her tightly so he could guide her movements and keep her balanced on top of him at the same time. In that process, her skirt began to bunch up around her waist, sliding inch by inch up over her thighs.

Even though he was already inside of her, seeing her skirt rise up like that did something for Clint. Bit by bit, he could see the smooth flesh of Amy's legs and thighs that had been denied to him before. There was a certain excitement that came along with finally getting what had once been forbidden. And when that forbidden fruit was as delectable as Amy's naked skin, that made the victory all the sweeter.

Finally, Amy reached down and pulled her skirts up so she could rock back and forth when Clint gave her a chance. Clutching the material to herself, Amy groaned loudly while riding his cock. Clint watched her face as she took him inside of her and then turned his eyes downward to glimpse the thatch of hair between her legs.

Amy's pubic hair was the same light brown color as the hair on her head. He couldn't resist moving his fingers down there to feel what appeared to be so soft and inviting. It felt like wispy down when Clint slid his fingers between Amy's legs. The lips of her vagina were warm and wet. When his thumb brushed against the sensitive nub of her clitoris, Clint felt every muscle in her body tense.

"Good Lord," she whispered between shuddering breaths. "Don't stop."

Not one to disappoint a lady, Clint kept one hand in that spot while using the other to guide Amy's hips back and forth in just the right rhythm. Amy straightened up and allowed herself to be led wherever Clint wanted to go. Since there was no way to get out of her skirt without breaking away from Clint, she gathered it around her and held it so it draped behind her back.

Clint felt the material fall onto his feet and lower legs. Now that the skirt was accounted for, Amy could free up both hands. She placed them on her knees, supporting her back as she bounced up and down on top of him. Finally, she moved her hands up over her body until she threaded her fingers through her hair.

Throughout the course of their lovemaking, Clint and Amy used practically every inch of that chaise lounge.

Clint shifted back and forth on the padded surface while Amy used the back and side rests as handholds while she climbed all over Clint's body.

Clint wasn't even aware of how much time had passed, but he knew by the screams and moans coming from Amy that she'd experienced several climaxes. He'd been brought to the brink several times himself, but had held off just because he didn't want the moment to end. They wound up in one position, however, that would have been impossible for any man to resist.

Sitting up with his back supported by the upright back of the chaise, Clint was fully reclined with both knees slightly bent. Amy sat on top of him, straddling him as before, but resting with one leg over the side of the chaise and the other resting along Clint's side.

Clint held onto her tight little bottom with both hands. From there, all he needed to do was pump his hips slightly up and down while Amy used her entire lower body to slide him in and out of her. It felt as though he plunged deeper into her every time and whenever their hips met, they both let out grateful sighs.

Finally, Clint started to feel the world spin around him as his own orgasm threatened to overtake him. When it came, he exploded inside of her, coaxing Amy into yet another climax as she felt his rigid length drive into her one last time.

"So," Amy said breathlessly as she collapsed onto the chaise lounge, "that's what these big funny-looking chairs are for."

ELEVEN

Bo Walsh had charged into The Lighthouse full of piss and vinegar. After an hour or so of getting blank stares and shrugs in response to all of his questions, the fire in his belly started to flicker out. At first, Bo had thought that he just needed to be a little more aggressive in his questioning. Then, he realized what the holdup truly was.

"Mister Walsh," the source of the holdup said, "I must say it's a surprise to see you. Not exactly a pleasant one, but a surprise all the same."

Fixing his eyes on the man dressed in the fancy tuxedo, Bo did his best to maintain his posture. "Hello, Karl. Nice work you've done to the place."

Karl glanced around at the casino area of the saloon as though he'd only just noticed that it was crammed full of paying customers. "Oh, you mean the remodeling? Yes, I guess you could say there was some good work to that end. I expected to quadruple my profits, but I only tripled them." With a smug grin, he added, "Such a disappointment."

Even though Red Parks was nowhere near the place, Bo could practically hear the fit Red would have thrown if Karl had said that to Red's face. For Bo, on the other hand, the only real annoyance was the smart-ass tone in Karl's voice.

"Have you seen The Lucky Lady in a while?" Bo asked.

Karl made a face as if he'd just smelled some rotten fish and replied, "No. Even if I did enjoy going to that type of place, I wouldn't have time since being a success takes up so very much of my time."

"What kind of place do you mean?"

"The kind that uses cheap bar fights as entertainment because the owner is too stupid to think of anything better and the whores are too ugly to turn more than a penny per fuck."

Now that did get Bo's blood running. The way Karl spat out his words, it was obvious that he was trying to rattle the man in front of him. Instead of snapping at the bait, Bo took a breath and forced himself to be the better man.

The last time he was at The Lighthouse, he'd blackened Karl's eye when the well-dressed man gave him lip. That time, just like this one, Bo had made the mistake of decking Karl inside his own place. Once the bouncers had shown up, Bo had been knocked around so badly that he barely remembered the pain. When he woke up, it was the next morning and Bo was in an alley by the wharves. No matter how good it would feel to crack his knuckles against Karl's face, Bo maintained his composure and resisted temptation.

"What's the matter, Bo?" Karl asked. "You look like you're about to burst."

Bo merely shrugged. The storm inside him was receding.

Karl raised his eyebrows and nodded. "I guess Red's put some time into training you properly. Oh well. I guess any dog can be trained."

The edges of Bo's discretion started to fray, but they held.

Sensing that he wasn't about to get under Bo's skin at that moment, Karl said, "I hear you've been storming around here asking questions. What is it you want?"

"You mean you'd help me if I told you?"

"If it would get you out of here any sooner, then yes. I'd see what I could do."

Bo's first instinct was to walk away from Karl since expecting any real aid from him would have been beyond stupid. But since Karl would only come right back at him again, Bo decided to play along if only to see where it would lead. "I heard Clint Adams is staying here," Bo said.

"Yes, he is. A man like him knows the best places to stay, which is why he's decided to st—"

"I'd like to see him," Bo interrupted.

His mouth still hanging open after being cut off, Karl took his time before answering. "I could send a message to his suite."

"You do that." Suddenly, Bo spotted something that caught his attention. Although the sight was a welcome one, he did his best to make sure Karl didn't notice any change in his face. Fortunately, the man in the tuxedo was too busy trying to keep his voice down to notice much of anything else.

"So tell me, Karl," Bo said before the other man could get another comment in. "Can't you run your own place well enough on your own without someone like Clint Adams around?"

When he responded, Karl's voice didn't have the refined texture it had started out with. Like sandpaper against wood, the meeting with Bo had worn away at his normally impenetrable veneer. "I can run this place just fine," he said in something just short of a snarl. "A hell of a lot better than your friend Red Parks ever could.

Unlike Red, I know this business and if he knew jack shit about anything at all, he would see the value of having men like Adams around."

"Is that so?"

"It is. He's drawing in more business than I know what to do with and all it costs me is a suite and a few free meals. Rough men like him draw trouble, but the moment that happens, I've got my own men to escort him out and keep him from ever coming back."

Karl stopped himself when he saw the smirk that was fighting to make its way onto Bo's face. Just then, the bottom of Karl's stomach dropped out and he spun around on his heels to come face to face with the very subject of his conversation.

Clint stood there with Amy on his arm, waiting patiently to be noticed. "Please," Clint said, "don't let me bother you."

"Mister Adams," Karl said, doing his best to gain back his former composure. "I hope you didn't mistake anything I said to this ruffian as any sort of bad reflection upon you."

"Of course not. I'm sure you were just talking and it didn't mean a thing."

Just then, the bartender jogged up behind Clint and tapped him on the shoulder. When Clint turned around, the barkeep was able to see who he was talking to and realized he'd just stumbled into a situation that he would have rather avoided.

"What is it?" Karl snapped at the barkeep.

"I, uhh, just needed to tell Mister Adams that someone wanted to have a word with him." The pause between breaths quickly became a very uncomfortable silence. "Actually, that's the man that wanted to talk to you, Clint," he added, pointing to Bo. "I guess I'll be going now."

The glare coming from Karl directed at the barkeep

had enough intensity behind it to act as a swift kick to the other man's backside. Once the bartender had hurried away, Karl plastered on a smile and looked back toward Clint. "Anything I can do for you, Mister Adams?"

Clint plastered on a smile as well. "There sure is. I need you to toss a few more of those free meals my way before I get too out of control and need to be tossed out into the street."

"Once again, Clint, I assure you I meant nothing by that when—"

Clint stopped him with a raised hand. "I'd prefer it if you called me Mister Adams."

"Oh. Of course."

"And I'd also like another free meal for this gentleman right here," Clint said, motioning toward Bo. When he saw the disgusted look on Karl's face, he asked, "Will that be a problem?"

"No," Karl forced himself to say. "Not at all."

Clint's wide, phony smile came back brighter than ever. "Great! I certainly appreciate it. You're one hell of a host, Karl. I'll be sure to tell all my rough, trouble-making friends about this place."

And with that, Clint, Amy and Bo all went off to enjoy their free meals.

TWELVE

Amy had wanted to ask Clint why he seemed so pleased to see Bo, but she didn't get a good opportunity. Between the tense exchange with Karl and the silence that followed, it seemed better for her to just keep quiet and go along with him rather than ask any questions. More than that, however, Clint just didn't seem too receptive to answering anything at that point in time.

None of that was because Clint seemed angry. In fact, it was quite the opposite. Clint didn't seem able to wipe the smile off his face even if he'd wanted to. But despite that smile, there was still something about him that made just going along with him all the wiser.

The three of them were shown to a table in the back of the dining room that had become Clint's normal spot for the meals taken at The Lighthouse. Once they were seated and the waiter left them alone to look over the menu, Clint finally let the facade he'd been wearing drop away. All in all, Amy decided she would have preferred the fake smile and quiet to the annoyed expression that replaced it.

"What an arrogant little prick," Clint grumbled. "I knew I was being used to draw business, but at least that asshole in a tuxedo could have appreciated it a bit more."

"He does have that way about him," Bo said.

Clint looked over to him and asked, "You know Karl?"

Nodding, Bo replied, "Yep. And he's driven out more than his share of good workers because he treated them more like pets than people. By the way," he added, offering his hand toward Clint, "my name's Bo Walsh."

"Clint Adams."

The two men shook hands, which was enough to get rid of the remaining tension that had been in the air.

Bo gave Amy a quick nod before turning back toward Clint. "I see you've already met my sister."

Clint's expression froze onto his face. Suddenly, it felt awkward to be sitting at that table with Bo. Most of that awkwardness came from the fact that Clint could still feel the chills that had gone up his spine after making love to Bo's sister. When he glanced over to Amy, Clint was just in time to see her glance down like a little girl who'd been caught being naughty.

"Yes," Clint said. "She didn't tell me her family would be coming for a visit, though."

If Bo noticed any of what was going on between Clint and Amy, he didn't give off the first clue. "Not the whole family," Bo said. "Just me. She said she could be a help to me in getting a sit-down with you, so I thought I'd give her a shot. Looks like she earned her keep."

"Yeah," Clint said. "I'd have to agree with you there."

Reaching over across the table, Bo patted his sister's hand and gave her an approving nod. It was at that moment that Clint decided the other man was oblivious to what had truly gone on with his sister. For the sake of making things go smoother, Clint decided to leave it that way.

Bo was the first one to steer things back in the proper direction. "First of all, let me just say it's an honor to meet you, Mister Adams."

"Just call me Clint."

"Sure. Thanks. My employer and I have heard a lot about you." Bo stopped for a moment to let that revelation sink in. When he saw absolutely no reaction from Clint, he cleared his throat and went on. "I know you're probably very busy, but I was hoping that you might hear me out. It's regarding a business proposition that I think you'll—"

"You might want to save your breath," Clint interrupted. "I hate to be rude, but I'm really not looking for any business proposals right now. To be honest, the main reason I looked interested was to get under Karl's skin. And, judging by the little tantrum he's still throwing over there, I'd say it worked. So why don't we just shoot the breeze and enjoy a good meal together?"

"I'd really like that, Clint. The only thing is that I really need to discuss this matter with you. It's pretty important."

Now that the aggravation of dealing with Karl was wearing off, Clint had been able to get a better look into Bo's eyes. He could see that there was indeed something big weighing on him. This was one of those moments that Clint wished he could be just a little more callous when it came to folks in need. It might have made him a colder person, but his life would sure have less bumps in it.

"All right," Clint said. "Since we're all here anyway, go ahead and say what's on your mind."

The relief on Bo's face was overwhelming and he let out a huge breath that must have been building up since Clint had first introduced himself. "That's great. I work for a man named Red Parks and he owns a place called The Lucky Lady."

"A saloon?"

"That's right."

Narrowing his eyes, Clint said, "This had better not be another scheme to use my name to attract business. I've had my fill of being an attraction for quite some time."

"Oh no, it's nothing like that." This time, it was Amy who cut in. When she saw the look on Clint's face at her sudden interest in the conversation, she shrugged and explained, "I meant to talk to you about this, but we didn't really have the time."

"No, we sure didn't."

"We may not be able to offer you all the benefits you'd get here," Bo said, taking back the reins from his sister, "but in the long-term, it could be a much sweeter deal."

"How so?"

"Excuse me," came a voice from over Clint's shoulder.

Clint didn't even have to turn around to know who was talking. "What do you want, Karl? I'm in the middle of a conversation."

"I was just . . . uh . . . checking to see if you needed anything."

"Nope. Just talking business with Bo here. You mind giving us some breathing room?"

The anger could be felt streaming from Karl like waves of heat emanating from his tuxedo. After he stalked away, he could still be seen lurking nearby to keep tabs on what was going on.

Clint saw all of this and smirked at Amy and Bo. "This just keeps getting better. I've been a wanted man before, but it was never half as enjoyable as this."

THIRTEEN

"Here's the real problem," Bo said once their drinks and some bread had been brought over to their table. "The Lucky Lady is a fine place. Actually, it could be the best place in town."

"And which town is that?" Clint asked.

"Crystall. It's not too far from here."

"Well, being the best place in any town doesn't sound like much of a problem to me."

"I said it could be the best. There's just one thing keeping it from being the best."

"And what's that?"

Bo tried to think of a good way to phrase it. Unable to come up with one, he shrugged and said, "It's a bloody mess. I swear we sweep up more teeth than dust from the floor every night. We could become a good stop for the professional gamblers, but they know better than to take any real money into a place like that. Red even tried getting some high-class singers and such to play there, but after one got shot in the middle of his number, word spread and we're lucky if we can get some two-cent whores to kick their heels up.

"And that just opens up a whole other mess of problems. Red had a few of his working girls turn up dead and that scares the rest of them away. Not to mention the ones that just didn't turn up." Bo shook his head and rubbed his hands over his eyes. "That just leaves liquor, cheap card games and fights to pass the time."

"Not a very good combination," Clint said. "That is, unless you're looking to add more plots to your town's boot hill."

"We didn't even have a boot hill until The Lucky Lady turned to shit," Amy said. When she saw the scolding look from her brother, she shrugged it off and looked away.

Apparently, Bo couldn't really think of a good comeback to her accusation so he just let it drop.

"Sounds like your boss may be better off if he just started over somewhere else," Clint said. "I'm not exactly in the saloon-keeping business."

"Red already sunk everything he owns into his place and with word spreading about The Lady, finding investors hasn't been too easy."

"Word's spread about a place in Crystall? I haven't even heard about that town until now," Clint pointed out, "not to mention a place called The Lucky Lady."

"Oh, word's spreading all right," Amy said. "I got here just ahead of my brother and have been making the rounds to all the saloons in San Francisco. Just about every place has stories going around that The Lucky Lady is practically a slaughterhouse that serves whiskey."

"How do things like that get around?" Clint asked. "I know gamblers and gunfighters get reputations. Even some towns have their reputations, but a saloon in some small town?"

"You want to know how that happens? All you have to do is look right over there." With that, Amy pointed straight back to Karl Patrice. "Karl and Red go way back. Once they parted ways, Karl took everything he learned from Red and turned it against him to keep Red down while he built himself up."

"Cutthroat business," Clint observed. "That's why I never really got into it."

"Karl's not our only problem," Bo said. "Red can handle him just fine. It's these assholes coming into The Lucky Lady like they own the place and using it as their own private shooting gallery. They started out squeezing us for protection money just like they squeezed everyone in town. Red paid them. He said it was just another price of doing business."

Clint hated to hear things like that, mainly because it was akin to a man letting a rat gnaw on his foot just so it would leave the rest of him alone. Men who demanded protection money were nothing but rats themselves and nobody liked a rat. Clint was certainly no exception to that rule.

"So what is it you want from me?" Clint asked. "I know most of the stories going around about me, but I don't hire out my gun."

"Oh, Red doesn't want any part of that." Suddenly, Bo's eyes widened as though he'd just remembered something important. His hand snapped into his jacket so quickly that it made Clint's arm twitch reflexively toward his Colt.

Clint gave Bo a moment before drawing his gun. When Bo's hand emerged from beneath his jacket, it was holding something much less threatening than a firearm. At least, it was less threatening in the short term.

"These papers are from Red," Bo told Clint. "He sent me out here to deliver them to you so you could take a look at his offer."

"You can write it up however you want," Clint warned before accepting the paper bundle. "I'm still not a hired gun."

"Red wants you to work for him, but only for a little

while. With you being a known man and all, having you around would make it easier for us to be rid of them that want to keep putting blood on The Lady's floor every night.

"That's not to say that your hands won't get dirty. This bunch wouldn't want to leave even if Jesus Christ came and asked them to. But Red wants to hire you on as a security council-eh-ter."

"Consultant?" Clint clarified.

Snapping his fingers, Bo said, "That's the word. Security consultant. I gather that's just a fancy word for someone who cracks the heads that needs cracking and keeps a place clean so the better folks won't be afraid to drop by."

Clint opened the bundle Bo handed to him and started leafing through the papers. By the looks of it, this Red Parks might have gone to law school before opening a saloon. Either that, or he had some high-priced counsel of his own to draw up the papers.

The bulk of the papers were contracts for service as well as a two-page letter from Red himself. So far, everything in the letter had already been said by Bo himself. There was one bit that caught Clint's eye, however, and he immediately shuffled through the contracts to make sure he'd read it correctly.

After finding what he was after, Clint put on his coolest poker face and glanced up at Bo. "So what's in it for me?"

"See, now that's the good part," Bo replied. "A man like yourself comes highly recommended and should ... uhh ... be compensated as such."

Clint nodded through Bo's pitch since it had obviously been spoonfed to him by his boss.

"Seeing as how you're so valuable and ... so ... good at what you—"

"Just cut to the deal, Bo," Clint pleaded.

"Red's offering part ownership in The Lucky Lady if you can clean it up for him."

"How much?"

"Fifteen percent."

Clint glanced down at the paper he'd found and then looked back up at Bo. "Try twenty-five percent."

"Oh, yeah. That was it."

Reading over that contract which outlined the details of the offer, Clint nodded and said, "Now that does sound interesting."

"So you'll do it?"

"I'll go to Crystall and talk to Red. After that, I'll decide if I take the job or not."

"That's great!"

"But there's one condition."

The happiness in Bo's eyes dimmed a bit when he heard that. "What condition?"

"I want to be there where you tell Karl I'm leaving."

FOURTEEN

It was just another night in the Lucky Lady Saloon.

Actually, the last few nights had been more active since Red was working without the help of one of his best men. With Bo gone, there was just one less barrier between himself and the rowdies that had made The Lady their home. Each night that went by was louder than the one before it until finally Red was about ready to yank his hair out by its roots.

It was only six o'clock and already things were looking worse. The regular filth had trudged in to make themselves comfortable while the few good patrons of the place were looking to make a quiet exit. As always, Red went over to those handful of locals who didn't want to tear up the place so he could bribe them with free drinks.

Part of him made Red feel bad for enticing good folks to stay when he knew damn well there was going to be trouble. But that part wasn't strong enough to keep him from heading over there with a smile on his face. This was, after all, only business.

"Howdy folks," Red said in a Texas drawl that he put on for just such occasions. He was a Texan, but he tended to lay the accent on a bit thick to put a smile on his customers' faces. Usually, it worked.

"Uh . . . hi, Red." Apparently, this wasn't one of those times.

"What's with the long faces?"

The customers were a group of four men who worked at a nearby shipping company. After having a few beers, they were making eyes toward the front door. None of them seemed too anxious to talk, but that was just out of respect for Red. They had other concerns as well, as was made clear by the nervous glances toward the loud gunmen who'd taken up at the bar.

"We were just about to head out," one of the locals said.

Red did a fairly good job of looking surprised when he said, "What? Really? But the night's still young. How about I pull up a chair, buy the next round and we can swap stories?"

"Maybe next time, Red."

"Aw, don't let those ol' boys scare you out of here. They're just full of hot wind. Kind of reminds me of this bunch I had to run out of my place in Amarillo."

As he spoke, Red pulled up a chair and was just about to sit down when he felt several sets of boots rattle the floorboards nearby. The steps were headed in his direction and when he turned around to take a look for himself, he was just in time to see a large figure dressed in gray reach out to yank the chair away from him.

"What's this you were saying?" the man in gray asked.

Red felt his stomach clench, but tried not to look like anything was amiss. His eyes darted around to get a look at the locals, but he saw that it was too late to salvage any business from them for the night. The four men were already stepping away. After only a few steps, they came into contact with some of the others that were with the man in gray.

"I was just talking, Lowell," Red said. "That's all. We're all just out for a good time and nobody needs to get bent out of shape."

Lowell might very well have been the source of the old saying referring to putting a dress on a pig. Despite the nice material or good cut of his gray suit, the man inside of it was still a pig. His face was twisted into a perpetual sneer and was covered with pockmarks deep enough to be craters. Scraggly, light blond hair poked up from his head like a fresh crop of weeds.

"Only one that's gonna get themselves bent is you," Lowell snorted. "That is, when I bend you around one of these posts and then bend both your arms back the wrong way."

Seeing that all eyes in the place were on him and Lowell, Red put on a thoroughly unconvincing smile and laughed weakly. "That's a good one, Lowell. You're such a kidder." Turning to the few good customers in the place, he added, "We always kid around like this. He's been coming in here for a good, long while."

None of the other customers were buying the line Red was trying to feed them. Even so, they weren't anxious to draw attention to themselves, either. That left them stuck right where they were; too nervous to stay and too hesitant to make a run for the door.

Lowell hooked his thumbs in the little pockets of his vest and leaned back like the dandy he thought he was. "Now that you mention it, we have been coming in here for a long time. We toss a lot of business your way and we barely get much more than the average cowboy that drags his carcass in here."

"I try to extend my courtesy to all my guests," Red pointed out.

"Then you must not see me and my friends here as guests because we don't get a damn bit of courtesy from you."

Plenty of things came to Red's mind. Unfortunately, he was certain not one of them would do him any good at that particular moment. "Tell you what, then. I'll set you up with some free drinks. In fact, a free drink for everyone!"

Red's offer sounded throughout the saloon like words shouted down an empty hall. Nobody responded to him and nobody dared to make a sound of their own. They were either too uncomfortable to speak or were waiting to follow Lowell's lead.

"Sounds like you don't got any takers on that one, Red. I'll bet right now you were wishing you'd treated me and my boys a little better."

The others standing around Lowell knew their cue when they heard it. They all took a step forward, converging on Red like a fist squeezing the life out of a mouse.

The front doors opened and shut, but only a few of the locals closest to them glanced in that direction. Red's view was blocked by the wall of bad intentions closing in on him in the form of gun hands forming a shoulder-to-shoulder barricade. Lowell only shifted slightly so he was sure his words reached back to the front of the room.

"The Lady's closed," Lowell grunted. "Go get your drink somewheres else. It'll be better than the slop they serve here anyhow."

One of Lowell's men tried to shove the new arrival back outside, but was knocked on his ass before he made it very far.

"That's funny," Clint said as he stepped over the man he'd just punched in the gut. "I heard a man could get some good beer in this place."

FIFTEEN

"Who the hell are you?" Lowell snarled as he wheeled around to get a look at who'd just knocked down one of his biggest men.

Clint had just been walking into the saloon when the hulking figure came rushing toward him. Like any big, dumb animal, there was a blankness in his eyes that Clint could see almost immediately. It was the look of someone too used to having people fall before him with little or no effort. It was the look of a fighter who hadn't gotten his ass kicked enough times to make him truly tough.

All Clint needed to do was twist his body to roll with a sloppy shove and then duck beneath a hasty punch. After that, he was staring at a wide-open target. The punch Clint threw was just strong enough to knock the wind out of the bigger man and when that man crumpled, Clint pushed him right over.

"Could be I was just looking for a drink when this one here tried to put his hands on me."

Lowell looked like a dog trying to figure out how a printing press worked. He squinted his eyes when he looked over at Clint and cocked his head at a strange angle. Finally, he just had to look away and glance over to someone he could figure out.

"Someone shut this asshole's mouth," Lowell barked to the closest of his cronies he could find.

There were a few of them around, but one of them seemed more than willing to oblige. When that one stepped up and offered his hand to the bigger man who was still trying to recover from the jab to his gut, his hand was swatted away.

"I can handle myself," the big guy said.

With all the wind back in his sails, the big man stood next to and slightly in front of the reinforcement that had been sent. Only a few moments had passed since Clint had walked into The Lucky Lady. In that time, Bo and Amy stepped in through the door to get a quick overview of what was going on.

"I should'a known," the big man said when he spotted Bo. "I was startin' to think you had enough sense to keep your face from being seen around here."

Even though Clint was standing in front of Bo, he could feel the hackles raising on the back of Bo's neck.

"I'm not the one that's unwelcome around here, Lowell," Bo said in a voice that was like tempered steel.

Standing between the two men, Clint felt like he'd been forgotten altogether. "So how about that drink?" Clint asked as a way to either break the tension or bring it to a head. "Am I going to get served or not?"

"Sure you'll get served," Lowell said. Snapping his fingers toward the other two men standing closer to Clint, he ordered, "Give our friends here a heaping serving of what they need."

His pride still aching from getting knocked down by a single punch, the bigger man cracked his knuckles and walked straight toward Clint. The other man who Lowell had sent over was right behind him, but knew better than to interfere in what the bigger fellow had planned.

Clint could read the big man like a book. Having honed that particular skill in countless card games, Clint had become somewhat of an expert in figuring out what someone else was going to do before that person even came to a definite decision. In a fight, that skill was even more valuable and men were less likely to try and hide their intentions.

Knowing just what he needed to do in order to get the response he needed, Clint waited until the big man started walking before giving him a smirk and a quick wink. Sure enough, that sent the big man straight over the edge and got him to charge forward like a crazed bull.

Clint stood his ground for a second or two, which was just enough time for the other man to fully commit to his attack. At the last possible second, Clint stepped aside so that he could watch the other man rush by. From there, he sent a quick, stabbing jab into the big man's ribs just for good measure.

Having become accustomed to fights breaking out at the drop of a hat, Bo had no trouble at all spurring himself into action. He was right there to cover Clint's back once the big man made his initial charge. The other guy sent by Lowell twisted around to grab hold of the nearest chair and got both hands wrapped around its back before he had Bo to contend with.

Bo placed his hand flat upon the back of the chair and pushed it down to prevent the other man from lifting it up. Balling his free hand into a fist, he snapped it forward and cracked it straight into the other man's jaw.

With all of that in motion, the only thing left was for the rest of the saloon to erupt into chaos. Lowell ran forward to back up the first two and the rest of his men came rolling in behind him. Clint remained focused on the big man for the moment because Amy was still fairly close by. Bo had his hands full since the man he'd been struggling with had managed to wrestle the chair from him.

"Aw shit," Red grumbled. "Here we go again."

SIXTEEN

Turning to one of his nearby workers, Red shouted, "What the hell do I pay you boys for? Get in there!"

Like troops swarming enemy lines, the rest of Red's male staff jumped into the fray. Some of them seemed more anxious than others, but none of them were newcomers to the game of busting heads. Soon, the air was filled with ladies' screams, curses from the men, chairs, bottles and just about anything else that could be picked up and tossed.

Clint reared back his arm to take a heartier swing at the big man and was caught by a surprisingly quick punch to the stomach. Even as he doubled over, he knew he was in trouble. There wasn't anything he could do to prevent what was coming, however, and was forced to take the big man's knee to his jaw.

Pain lanced through Clint's head, but he was quick enough to turn away at the last moment. Although that kept his jaw from getting busted, it didn't make it hurt any less. The big man's knee slammed into Clint's face like a tree trunk. For a moment, all Clint could see was some sparkling bits of light through a black fog. After sucking in a quick breath and shaking his head he felt better, but that only lasted until he was blindsided by a punch thrown from outside his field of vision.

Rolling with the punch as much as he could, Clint used that momentum to turn himself toward whoever had hit him so he could deal with that new threat. The other guy was a scrawny little punk with a face full of wiry black whiskers. That was all Clint saw before he slammed his own fist into that newest face.

The wiry fellow went over with a curse, freeing Clint up to dodge another powerful swing from the big man. Watching the bigger man move, Clint knew the punch to the ribs had definitely had an effect. He used that to his advantage by holding back and dodging the next few swings until he spotted the opening he needed.

That opportunity came when the big man reared back and took a swing that was aimed at Clint's chin. If he hadn't ducked down at the right time, Clint knew damn well that his head might have been knocked clean off his shoulders. As it was, he felt the rush of air as the other man's arm passed over his head, giving Clint a prime view of the same set of ribs he'd punched before.

This time, Clint put some more steam into his arm as he brought it up toward the same area he'd hit before. He also drove upward with his legs and even twisted his hips into it so all of that force was behind that single punch. When it landed, Clint could feel bones snapping. He drove his knuckles in even further, however, wanting to put the big man out for good before a lucky shot knocked Clint into next week.

For a moment, Clint thought he hadn't gotten the job done after all. After the punch had plowed through his ribs, the big man twisted away and clenched his side with his arm. His eyes were bright with pure rage and when he tried to take a breath, the pain he felt was just more fuel on the fire.

Reaching out with his other hand, the big man made a

straight grab for Clint's throat. Clint was so close to him that there was no way he could miss.

Feeling the thick, sausage-like fingers clamp around his windpipe, Clint tried to pull the big man's hand away. But in the space of a second or two, he could already feel his lungs straining for air and his balance starting to falter.

"Son . . . son of a b—" was all the big man got out. The words were forced and his voice sounded more like a wheezing grunt than actual speech. The effort of trying to talk with those busted ribs was too much for him and soon, the big man was unable to keep his knees from buckling.

The moment he felt the other man's strength starting to fade, Clint pulled himself out of the grip locked around his throat and took a step back. Although the big man's body still wanted to fight, his eyes were already empty and it was obvious there was no more steam in his engine. Placing his finger flat against the bigger man's forehead, Clint pushed him over and listened to the thump that rattled the floorboards.

Amy watched all of this from the spot she'd chosen. It seemed like the safest place she could find and was situated behind a large shelf that was used mainly to store linens and eating utensils. Every so often, she thought someone was coming for her, but that person kept right on going. There was plenty more going on out there, after all, and she pretty much went unnoticed.

With the big man down and Bo taking on the other one that had been closest to the door, the way was left open for customers to get out of the saloon altogether. They rushed for the exit at the first opportunity and damn near trampled Clint in the process.

Acting on reflex, Clint almost took a swing at someone rushing straight at him, but he paused long enough to see that the person was just trying to get out. He stepped aside and let the people get by, which didn't seem to go over too well with an older-looking gentleman running after them.

"Hold on, now!" Red shouted. "No need to clear out. This is under control."

Even as he said that, he was nearly taken off his feet by a chair that was swung at chest level. Instincts sharpened after being in way too many brawls bought Red enough time to sidestep the incoming chair and still rush in the wake of the customers.

"Seriously, folks," Red pleaded. "This is just a little scuffle. No need to leave so early in the night. Free drinks! Don't forget about the free drinks!"

A rough hand slapped against Red's back, nearly forcing him facedown onto the bar. Heavy steps made their way behind him and kept right on going. For the most part, the ruckus had died down to a few thumps and the occasional tinkle of broken glass being scattered.

"We'll be back for them free drinks," Lowell said, wiping some blood from the corner of his mouth as he walked toward the door. "Don't you worry about that."

The fight ended like a squall that had just rained itself out. Lowell and his men either made their way to the door or scooped up the ones who needed help getting there. Everyone else stayed ready to start the fight anew, but breathed a collective sigh of relief once they knew it was over.

Smirking despite the blood draining out of his nose, Bo looked over to Clint and said, "Now aren't you glad you decided to come?"

SEVENTEEN

With all the things he'd heard during the trip from San Francisco, Clint hadn't been too surprised to be involved in a fight less than a minute after he walked into The Lucky Lady. What did surprise him was just how quickly the saloon recovered from the brawl. In no time at all, the workers had most of the broken wood and glass swept up and were setting up a fresh round of drinks for the few customers who had chosen to stay.

Red was most affected by what had happened. He walked around the saloon, fussing over this broken glass or that broken chair, cursing the same couple of names over and over again. Clint couldn't make out more than a few words since the older man was too upset to be coherent. So, like Amy and Bo, Clint waited for Red to cool off a bit before trying to strike up a conversation.

Suddenly, Red looked up at the three new arrivals as though they'd just dropped down from the sky. "Bo! Come over here. Is that who I think it is?"

Bo dusted himself off and righted a table that had been knocked over sometime during the brawl. "Yeah, it is. Red Parks, meet Clint Adams."

At that moment, Red acted as though he was walking

through his saloon in the middle of its prime. He stepped over the glass and debris without stumbling once and made it to Clint with his hand open and extended. "Clint Adams, it sure is a pleasure to see you."

"Same here," Clint replied. "Although I am used to getting a little warmer of a reception."

Wincing as though he thought there was a chance that Clint might not have noticed the mess around him, Red said, "Sorry about that, but things can get a bit rough around here. Did Bo tell you much about my situation here?"

"Oh, he said it was rough, but there's nothing like seeing something for yourself to get the big picture."

"Now that you did get a look-see, I'll bet you're just looking to get the hell out of here."

"The thought did cross my mind," Clint admitted. "But since I came all this way, I might as well hear you out."

"You're a man among men, Clint. I truly mean that."

Now that there wasn't anything swinging toward his skull, Clint had to admit that The Lucky Lady was a damn fine saloon. Looking past the mess that was quickly being cleared away, the place truly was impressive. The stage and orchestra pit were empty at the moment, but it didn't take much imagination to envision how breathtaking they would be once they were full. Despite the fact that plenty of glasses and bottles had been broken, there were still plenty left behind the bar and only a small fraction of the card tables had sustained much real damage.

"I hear you got a look at The Lighthouse when you were in San Francisco," Red said as he stepped behind the bar and helped himself to a bottle and a pair of glasses.

Clint nodded. "I sure did. It's one hell of a place, but I've got to admit that this isn't anything to sneeze at either."

"I appreciate that. Considering how you got your first look at her, I take that as a big compliment for my Lucky

Lady." He filled both glasses with whiskey and slid one across the bar toward Clint. "For your time."

"You think I could trouble you for a beer?" Clint asked. "That's more my style."

"Sure, sure. Whatever you need."

Bo stepped up to the bar and stood next to Clint. With a nod, he took the glass that Clint had refused and tossed the whiskey back in one shot.

Moments after Bo's empty glass touched down onto the bar, a mug filled with beer was set down right beside it. Clint picked up the mug and took a drink. Although his mouth was a bit tender from the knocks he'd taken, the discomfort wasn't enough to keep him from drinking.

"So what did Bo tell you?" Red asked. "Hopefully he didn't leave too much unsaid."

"He told me you're in the market for a new head of security and that you think I could be the man you're after."

Red nodded and sipped his whiskey. "So far so good."

"He also told me that you've got a problem with some men who think you need to pay them to keep yourself from getting turned out every other night."

"That's a fact. Now, Clint, you've got to know that I've been in this business for some time and I know how things work. There's always men out there trying to collect and usually it's better off just to pay them. But there's some men who are more like coyotes than men. You feed them once and they come back again and again, wanting more each time. You know what I mean?"

The truth of the matter was that Clint knew such men like the back of his own hand. They were always the ones coming after innocent folks just because there wasn't anyone to stand up to them. The comparison to coyotes wasn't too far off the mark. The only sad part about it was that oftentimes, men like that seemed to outnumber coyotes two-to-one.

"Yeah," Clint said, avoiding the rest that flowed through his mind. "I know what you mean."

"Then you probably know men like that don't hit just one place out of an entire town for no reason."

Clint's eyes snapped up after taking a sip from his beer. "What are you saying? These men only expect protection from you?"

"No, the whole town pays. Some more than others, but we all pay. What I'm saying is that I get squeezed more than anyone else and it's not just because I own this here place."

"Then why is it?"

"That," Red said while slamming his glass down onto the bar, "is why I need someone like you to come work for me on this instead of just some idiot with a gun. So, Clint. You think you can take this job?"

Looking around at the mess that was almost cleaned up and knowing it wasn't going to be the last time he got a punch thrown at him in the very near future, Clint shrugged. "Will I get a place to stay and meals while I'm here?"

"There's a fine room upstairs and my cook's the best in town."

"Then I guess you can count me in."

EIGHTEEN

Sometimes, a man just had to listen to his gut instead of his head.

This, Clint knew, was most definitely one of those times. There were plenty of reasons to just finish his free beer, walk outside and ride Eclipse straight out of Crystall, California. Not the least of those reasons was that doing so would just make his life a hell of a lot easier. He'd already gotten into a fight and he was certainly on the bad side of those men that had stalked out of The Lucky Lady afterward.

But there were also some good reasons for him to stay. After leaving The Lighthouse in a way to sufficiently piss off that arrogant prick Karl Patrice, Clint needed to look for those to make sure he wasn't making a mistake. Clint got the feeling that Red was in way over his head. That was just Clint's reflexive thought since he'd seen the fire in Lowell's eyes. There was more there than just someone trying to stir up shit.

Something else was going on and it wouldn't be long before someone truly got hurt. Clint had seen it too many times to know the problem would just go away or burn itself out like so many others. Little fires had a tendency to turn into big fires and there was already a good-sized blaze roaring in The Lucky Lady.

Plus there was the matter of doing a job for the oldest reason in the history of working: to get paid. As much as he liked living free and going wherever he felt himself being drawn, Clint was all too aware that such a life didn't come for free.

One of the best ways to fund his travels was to make smart investments. Clint already owned bits and pieces of restaurants, casinos and mines across the entire country. He'd started off being stuck with his shares as payment for helping out people when they needed him the most. Over time, those bits and pieces had treated him pretty well and were much more reliable than relying on his luck at cards to pay for his room and board.

Sitting in The Lucky Lady, nursing his second beer, Clint thought about all of this as a way to justify what he'd already agreed to do. All too often, he felt like a sucker for putting his life on the line to help people he'd never even met. Sure, that was the right thing to do, but his life was still on the line. He shook his head and wondered when that helpful streak of his would turn around and bite him on the ass.

"You look like you've got a lot on your mind," a familiar voice said from over Clint's shoulder. "Mind if I sit down?"

"Sure, Bo. Take a load off."

Bo eased himself into the seat next to Clint and set his mug of beer on the table. For a moment, both men sat there as though they needed to catch their breath. It had been a while since the brawl, but not long enough for their bruises to stop hurting just yet.

"The Lucky Lady," Bo said while shaking his head. "Sometimes I wonder if Red should have picked a more appropriate name."

Clint smirked. "I guess that depends on how everything turns out."

"You're probably right." After taking another sip and wiping the foam from his mouth with the back of his hand, Bo added, "With you in the mix, I'd say we got a better chance of living up to that luck. Lord knows we earned it."

After a few more sips, both of them had emptied their mugs. A pretty waitress came over to give them a refill and sauntered back to the bar so they could talk in peace.

"Where's Amy?" Clint asked. "I haven't seen her since the dust settled in here."

"Oh, I sent her to my grandpappy's place in Reno."

"Reno? Don't you have a place to stay in town?"

"Sure, but things may be getting a little rough. She wanted to stay, but even she knows how things are gonna be." Shifting in his seat, Bo added, "That's kinda what I wanted to talk to you about."

"Good, because that's kinda what I wanted to ask you about."

"Heh. There ain't no flies on you, I suppose."

"No," Clint replied. "There aren't. Not when it comes to dealing with a blood feud. I've seen too many of them to have one get by me."

"Blood feud? I never really thought of it like that."

"Maybe not. But does that seem out of line?"

Bo took another drink and mulled it over. The process seemed like a genuine effort on his part, but ended with a simple shrug. "Not out of line, exactly. There sure as hell ain't any love lost between Dutch and Red."

"There we go," Clint said, leaning back while lifting his mug. "Now we're making some progress. Who's Dutch?"

"Dutch Wilson is the fella I was telling you about before who takes payment from every business in town that makes any sort of profit. He's got some men working for him that make his word the law around here."

"And what about the real town law?"

Again, Bo shrugged. "Marshal Camms isn't a bad man, exactly, but he just don't have as much pull as Dutch around here. He's only got a few deputies and every last one of them knows it's better to just leave Dutch be rather than go against his hired guns.

"For the most part, Dutch is pretty careful about the laws he breaks. There ain't much to connect him to what he does. Well, not officially anyway."

"You know about what he does," Clint pointed out. "Sounds to me like plenty of folks know."

"Knowing about it is one thing," Bo said. "Doing anything about it is something else altogether. Besides, Dutch does some good for people every now and then and doesn't ask much in return."

"That doesn't seem to be what Red thinks."

"And that brings us right back to that blood feud you mentioned. Whatever is brewing between them two does seem like something different than the rest. I can tell you this much, though: whatever it is started way before I was on Red's payroll."

Clint nodded and drained a good portion of his beer with a healthy swallow. Setting the mug down solidly, he pushed away from the table and got to his feet. "Well, since I'm in this, I might as well get started."

"So you don't mind dealing with Dutch and his crew?"

"The deal was for me to get this saloon back into shape," Clint pointed out. "That's what I aim to do. As for the rest of all that, I'll just have to take it as it comes."

"It'll be coming, all right," Bo said. "Don't forget I warned you. It'll sure as hell be coming."

NINETEEN

Red couldn't have been happier when Clint told him he was accepting the job. The saloon owner practically did a dance since he was so certain that Clint would have the sense to get out while he could, especially after getting in a fight upon arrival. But his joy was tempered quickly enough once he sat down and had a talk with Clint.

Laying it all down for him, Clint set out the limits of what he was going to do to earn his payment. Even though it had been said plenty of times, he needed to make sure that Red wasn't thinking he was hiring Clint's gun. Only his services were being offered and that would have to be enough.

Apparently, that was plenty.

"So, we've got a deal?" Clint asked.

Extending his hand, Red nodded once and said, "We've got a deal."

"Great. Now let's get started. I want to talk with everyone who works here."

"Just name the time and place."

The time was about an hour after Clint's talk with Red. The place was in the main room of The Lucky Lady. It

76

was early afternoon, so it wasn't too hard to close the bar down for the length of the meeting. All the staff gathered there, excluding only those who dealt specifically with the parts of the place that didn't concern drinking, gambling or entertainment.

"All right," Red said as he walked up and down in front of his staff. "I wanted to get you all together here so I could introduce you to Clint Adams. He'll be working with us for a while to see if we can't get this place running the way it's supposed to."

One of the men, a scrawny fellow with thinning black hair, looked around at everyone in the room. "Where's Trudy and her girls?"

"Trudy's in charge of keeping the hotel rooms clean as well as the cooking staff," Red explained to Clint. Turning to the scrawny fellow, he said, "The problems we have don't concern cooks or maids."

"Oh, so you're saying we're the problem?" the scrawny fellow said, his voice and face reflecting the personal slight he felt.

Clint stepped up and said, "Nobody's saying you people are the main problems we have. But Red's right. The problem isn't with the hotel rooms and it isn't with the food. Can one of you name a time when there was a fight over some undercooked steak or dirty bed sheets?"

Clint looked around at all the faces staring back at him. The truth of the matter was that he didn't know if there had been any fights about such trivial things. He needed to get everyone in line and that little bluff was the first thing that had come to mind. Fortunately, Lady Luck seemed to favor that quick decision because nobody had anything else to say.

"The problem," Clint continued once he saw there was no more resistance just then, "is that the same bunch of assholes walk in here and stir up the shit. How many of you know who I am?"

Just about everyone there nodded, raised their hands, or gave some other form of acknowledgement.

"From what most of you have heard about me, you must know that I've had plenty of experience in dealing with assholes with bad manners."

That got a laugh from the people in the room, who all seemed to look at Clint more favorably because of it.

"The assholes that walk in here and cause trouble aren't much different than plenty of others I've met all across this country and a few others," Clint continued. "They do what they do mainly because they know they can get a way with it. I don't know if it's because the law doesn't care to step in or if Dutch Wilson just thinks he's the Second Coming, but there's some reason that they think they can get away with all this."

When he said that last part, Clint motioned around toward the stack of broken furniture piled behind the bar, which was the only visible reminder of the most recent fracas. "I can't say what that reason is just yet, but I aim to find out. I can also tell you that I don't think it'll be all that difficult of a job."

As he was talking, Clint walked back and forth in front of the gathered staff. Red stayed right beside him, but allowed Clint to talk without interruption. When he stopped talking, Clint also stopped walking. He wound up in front of a group of burly young guys who'd kept themselves clustered together.

"You three," Clint said, looking at each member of the group in turn. "What do you guys do here?"

The biggest of the bunch was also the spokesman. "We're security."

"Were you working earlier when this last fight broke out?"

"Yeah. Two of us was."

"Where were you?"

"Huh?"

"I was there too," Clint said. "And I don't recall seeing any of you get your hands dirty once the punches started to fly. Why is that?"

"Maybe your eyes ain't too good," the man snarled.

Clint nodded slowly. "That could be." Turning to one of the other burly men hired on for their fists, Clint said, "You were there. I remember you."

"Yes, sir," the barrel-chested man said.

"Did you see any of these three in that scrape?"

The barrel-chested man turned to make sure he looked at the group when he answered, "No sir. I didn't."

"What about you, Red? Did you see them there?"

"Nope. I sure didn't."

"Then that makes it easy. I think we need to cut some dead weight, so let's start with you."

"You ain't our employer," the spokesman for the other two said. "You can't—"

"But I can," Red interrupted. "Get out of here."

All three of them glared at Red and Clint in turn, spat up juicy wads onto the floor and then headed for the door. Once the resounding slam of their departure cleared the air, the room was overwhelmingly silent.

"Men like Dutch Wilson and the punks he hires only do as much as they think they can get away with," Clint said. "I'm here to be the man who says they can't get away with it anymore. This doesn't have to get ugly. Sometimes, all it takes is a strong hand from the outside and I guess that's me for the time being.

"I know going against someone with backing isn't easy, but now all of you in this room have me to back you. I'm sure there'll be a fuss at first, but this isn't exactly a war. You all just do your jobs and if there's any more trouble like there was this last time, just follow my lead. If any of you have any questions, I'll do my best to help you out."

Red stepped up and said, "It was just plain luck that

Clint was in the area and I heard about him because of Karl Patrice's big mouth."

The mention of Karl's name was enough to get a scowl from just about everyone else in the room.

"Now that Mister Adams is here," Red went on to say, "I think we should see what we can do to salvage this place before it gets sucked under. If for no other reason, we can at least do it to spite that asshole, Patrice."

Everyone seemed to get a kick out of that. Everyone, that is, except for that barrel-chested man sitting not too far from where Clint was standing. There was still some hesitance in his eyes as he looked to Clint and asked, "Things'll get worse before they get better. What happens then?"

"Then," Clint said to that man as well as everyone else, "I'll show you how to take out the trash."

TWENTY

It was another night at The Lucky Lady Saloon.

Although there weren't many differences on the outside, there were enough to separate that night from just any other typical night. First off, even though the security staff was stronger than most other saloons, they were still light by a few men. Those faces were missed by the regular crowd, but none of those locals seemed to be disappointed by the three men's absence.

Clint sat at the bar and kept his eyes on the front door when he wasn't glancing around at the rest of the room. He sat where he could see the most of the saloon as well as what he gathered were the trouble spots. His reasoning was that as long as he could tell who was entering the place, he could keep the wrong people from where they weren't supposed to be.

It was a reasonable enough thought and seemed easy enough to pull off. At least, it seemed easy when the night first got started.

Once the people started to flow through the doors and there was more to attract Clint's attention, he got a genuine feel for just how big a place The Lucy Lady truly was. Unlike most saloons that were only one room, the

Lady had three main areas for him to watch. There was the lobby and front door area which wasn't far from the bar. The casino branched off from there and the stage wasn't too far from that.

Clint's main concerns were the bar and gambling areas since that was where folks tended to get more riled up. But even trying to keep tabs on those two places became a chore once the entire place started to get stuffed to the rafters.

"Hell of a night, isn't it?" Red said through a beaming smile as he sauntered up to where Clint was standing.

Clint nodded, not at all surprised that the man charging for the drinks would be so tickled at such a crowd. From where Clint was standing, on the other hand, there wasn't a whole lot to make him smile.

"Yeah," Clint said. "Hell of a night."

One thing Clint had noticed before was catching his eye even more. At first, he thought some of the locals were just looking his way because he was an unfamiliar face. Now, he could tell that there was definitely more to it than that.

"Is the crowd normally this big, Red?"

Grinning like a proud papa, Red had his thumbs hooked through his suspenders and was rocking back and forth on his heels. "Nope. Not in a long time."

Clint nodded, giving it a few moments before he asked, "Any idea why so many of your customers look at me like I'm on stage?"

The smile froze on Red's face, but that was because the rest of him had frozen up as well. He became still as a statue and even caught himself perched on his tiptoes at the forward pinnacle of his rocking. Slowly, he turned his eyes toward Clint. "I know what you're thinking."

"I'll just bet you do," Clint said.

"I didn't go around flapping my gums the way Karl did about you being here."

"Are you sure about that?"

"Well, maybe I told a few folks that you might be coming. But that's not the same thing. I wasn't even sure Bo would be able to find you or if you'd even take the job."

Clint stopped him before Red could take a breath and string together another batch of apologies. "Just keep focused on what I'm doing here. If I'm going to be part owner of this place, I sure as hell don't want to see my investment go under because of some big-mouthed assholes."

Hearing the mention of the share he'd promised in return for Clint's services was like a splash of cold water on Red's face. It brought him back to the problem at hand and it brought him back real quickly. That was exactly what Clint had been hoping to do.

"You're right," Red said with a nod. "I should keep my eyes off the till and on the thorns in my side." With that, Red turned to Clint wearing a somewhat sheepish expression and added, "But, as a partial partner in this particular establishment, you've got to admit that it's pretty damn fine to see so much business in here."

Oddly enough, even though he knew the deal Red had offered and had signed the contracts himself, Clint hadn't really been thinking about the money aspect of the job. With all that lay in front of him, thinking about the reward was like focusing too hard on where to settle in gold country when the wagons weren't even through Nebraska.

Taking a moment to think about it now, however, Clint had to admit that Red made a good point. When he looked around, Clint took in the sight of the crowd as a whole instead of looking at each individual face for signs of trouble. He slipped into the role of businessman rather than security consultant and quickly found a smile gliding onto his face.

"Business is good, isn't it?" Clint said.

"Yeah," Red answered, seeing that his point had been made. "It sure is."

"What kind of money are we looking at here?"

"Let's just say I made a good living before this place started taking its downturn. Even when things were bad, I was still getting by. I'll let you flip through the books whenever you like, but I'll tell you one thing for certain. If things keep up half this well, we'll both be happy men."

Clint wasn't a greedy man. He'd always considered money to be just another necessity. Like food or water, money was something nearly every man needed to survive in the world. There were men who lived off the land, but Clint wasn't exactly that sort either. Most of the time, he thought money was a way most people kept score.

With all that in mind, Clint still felt a rush of excitement when he got a look at all the folks walking into The Lucky Lady. His smile grew wider when he saw them all drinking, eating, gambling and signing the register for one of the upstairs rooms.

Money was still just a necessity, like food or water, but it was still nice to sit down to a feast every once in a while.

"Aw, shit," came Red's voice like a hammer to shatter the good mood Clint had been working himself into.

Snapping right back into his more focused train of thought, Clint snapped his head toward the saloon owner and asked, "What is it?"

"Remember those thorns in my side we were talking about before?"

"Yeah."

"Well, they just walked in."

TWENTY-ONE

There were six thorns in all. Clint recognized three of them right away as some of the men that had stirred up the fight that had greeted him when he'd first arrived. Only one of those three walked toward the front of the new group. That one had been the leader before, but this time he walked behind another man the way a lieutenant deferred to a general.

"All right," Clint said without taking his eyes off the men gathering in the lobby and looking into the larger room with the bar. "How about you tell me a bit about these thorns before I walk into the patch this time."

Red was close by, focusing even more intently on the rough-looking men. "See that one in the front? That's Wade. He and Dutch are so close they're practically the same person. The one right next to him is Lowell."

"Yeah. We've met."

"The others are guns hired on by Dutch to collect his money and make life miserable for them that don't pay."

"Do they have names?"

In response to that question, Red merely shrugged. "When someone's sticking a gun in your face and telling you to hand over your hard-earned money, I don't really stop and think to ask for their names."

"Good point."

"Everyone around here just calls them the Enforcers because that's all they do. They enforce what Dutch and Wade want and don't think much farther beyond that."

Listening to Red talk, Clint watched as Wade, Lowell and the Enforcers strutted into the main room as if they were the ones who owned the place. The two leaders looked around, nodding happily very much the way Clint and Red had been nodding before. At that moment, Clint got a taste of the frustration and anger that Red must have been feeling this entire time.

Those thugs were happy because they knew there was more money available for them to steal. There was no question in their minds as to whether or not they would get paid. There was no gray area as to whether or not it mattered that they'd earned a penny of the till. They were going to take what they wanted and that was all there was to it.

At least, that was what they were thinking. Clint knew that much as certainly as if he could read their little minds. He could see their intentions like writing scrawled across their faces, only there was one big difference between what they thought and how things would actually turn out: Clint wasn't about to just roll over and play along with their demands.

He wasn't about to be intimidated and he sure as hell wasn't going to be pushed around by some group of assholes carrying guns.

And they were carrying guns; every last one of them. Clint picked out the iron on each man's hip in a matter of seconds. Not only was the group heeled, but the look in their eyes told him they would have no problem drawing those pistols and putting them to use.

That was all right. Clint was as familiar with being in

that situation as he was with sitting at a card table.

"I want you to stay here," Clint told Red.

"But I'm the one that they want to talk to. I should probably—"

"They also want you to hand over the night's profits. Are you going to oblige them on that account as well?"

Red thought about that for about a second and a half. In that time, he sucked in a breath and steeled himself. Shaking his head one time, he said, "No, sir. They're not getting another dime out of me."

Clint patted Red on the shoulder. "Good. Then you hold back and let me have a talk with them. That's why you hired me on, isn't it?"

"Yeah," Red said with no small amount of relief. "It is. But I want to do something more than that. This is my place, after all. I should do something more than just sit back and watch."

"You want to do something? Make sure that the rest of your staff is acting the way we discussed earlier and that they're ready to follow my lead. That'll be the biggest help you can give me."

"All right. I can do that."

As Clint started walking toward the front of the room, Red was moving as well. The owner of the place moved away to quickly tend to his workers and put some boot to backside if necessary. Clint was too focused to notice exactly where Red went because his attention had settled squarely on the man at the front of the group.

Wade had spotted him.

The tall, gray-haired man stepped forward as his lips curled up into a cold, sorry excuse for a smile. The expression on his face was more of a scowl and his eyes were like hunks of lifeless glass set beneath a hooded brow. He walked with purpose and confidence, knowing without having to see that his men were all behind him.

Lowell had a bit of confidence on his face as well, but

that stemmed mostly from the company he kept. Even
from across the room, Clint could see that one's resolve
was already rattled now that he saw that Clint was still in
The Lucky Lady.

Leaning over toward Wade, Lowell's lips moved in a
whisper as he spoke quick words into the other man's ear.
Taking in the words without breaking stride, Wade nodded slightly as his eyes narrowed and fixed even more
solidly onto Clint.

Fully aware of all that was going on in the space of
those few seconds, Clint made sure to keep his eyes on
target as well and keep his expression cool and controlled.
Just because Clint didn't think of himself as a gunfighter,
that didn't mean he wasn't fully versed in every aspect of
that sort of life. In his years, he'd been thrown into the
mix more times than he could count and he knew only
too well just how important every aspect of that particular
dance truly was.

When tensions were high and nerves were frayed,
every glance was important. Every movement made a difference just like every twitch of an eye could wind up
being a man's last. Judging by how Wade measured his
motions and controlled his own expression, the gray-
haired man was fully versed in those nuances as well.

As he crossed that room, Clint felt as though everyone
else inside of the place had faded away. The noise that
filled every bit of air inside the bustling saloon faded as
well in his ears, as every one of his senses fixed upon a
specific point.

. Wade was at that point and the rest of his men were
close by. Clint knew better than to allow himself to be
diverted, but he'd also summed up that Wade was indeed
the point of focus and the rest of the Enforcers were just
dangerous second stringers in comparison.

Someone else caught Clint's eye as well and that fact
came as something of a surprise to him. Keeping himself

so focused, he would have thought it impossible to be distracted. But distraction didn't exactly seem to cover it. Instead, he seemed more to have just noticed something else that was equally important.

The blonde was standing at the front end of the bar, her long golden hair flowing over one shoulder like a cascade of morning light. She was stunning in her own right, but what had caught Clint's eye was the way she seemed to be watching him and Wade with the same amount of intensity as the two men glared at each other.

She watched them walk closer to one another, fully aware of the tension building between them, but without being affected by it. Instead, she watched the way she might watch a bullfight. Despite the fact that she knew how dangerous the situation was, she wasn't about to look away.

There was something about that blonde besides just an incredibly beautiful face. Something in her eyes told Clint that she was no stranger to trouble and may even have some hand to play in the trouble brewing inside The Lucky Lady.

Unfortunately, the blonde would have to wait. Clint had bigger troubles to tend to and when he came to a stop, he was staring that trouble right in the eyes.

TWENTY-TWO

"That's him, Wade," Lowell said as his eyes nervously twitched between Clint and the gray-haired man. "That's the one I told you about."

One of the others behind Wade and Lowell nodded also. "Yeah. That's him all right."

"Shut up," Wade said. "The both of you. Can't you see I'm trying to introduce myself to this new friend of mine?"

Clint stood right where he was and let the other men talk themselves out. He knew there was going to be some kind of chatter and he decided to just wait it out until it was time to get down to business. By the looks of things, it seemed that Wade was thinking along the same lines.

"My name's Wade," he said, extending a hand to Clint. "I hope my partners here didn't make a bad impression on you before. We don't have anything against regular folk."

Clint's eyes darted down to look at the hand being offered to him and then back up at Wade's face. He shook hands, but made it brief. All the while, Clint was ready for some move to be made. Nothing came, but he could feel the tension in the gray-haired man's muscles as well, making them both seem like coiled springs.

"Clint Adams."

"Ah, so it really is you. I heard someone mention yer name, but didn't think much of it. No offense meant, but there's a lot of people who'd rather try to be someone they're not rather than face the music that's playin'."

"What can I get for you?" Clint asked, his face as cold as the side of a mountain.

Wade looked around. "How about a drink? This here is a bar, ain't it? Does everyone that comes in here looking for some liquor get greeted like this by the great Gunsmith himself?"

"No. Just the ones who took a swing at me the last time I ran into them."

Lowell twitched when he heard that. He tried to put some fierceness into his eyes to cover it up, but there was no painting over the initial panic that had been there before.

"Is that true, Lowell?" Wade asked, turning a stern expression toward the man right beside him.

"Must'a been a misunderstanding," Lowell said in a tone dripping with smug sarcasm.

Wade turned back to Clint and shrugged. "There. You see? It was a misunderstanding. Now how about them drinks?"

"First of all," Clint said, "how about you fellas take them guns off and leave them with the barkeep?"

Wade's smile faded, leaving the rest of his face as cold as his eyes. "Why would we do that?"

"Because you're just here for drinks."

"I see plenty of other folks around here that're heeled. What makes me and my boys so special?"

"Because we're still cleaning up the damage your boys did to this place not too long ago. That makes you a special case and if you don't like it, I hear there's a nice little saloon just down the street."

Nodding as he listened to Clint speak, Wade seemed to move forward without taking a step toward Clint. He only leaned in an inch or two, but he did it with such deliberation that the motion seemed more like a slow pounce.

Clint steeled himself as Wade inched closer. The feeling he got off the gray-haired man was the same as if he was standing too close to a rattler that was about to snap out and sink its fangs in.

"You sure you want to start this, Adams?" Wade asked in a voice that sounded like two rocks grinding together.

"I'm not starting anything. You and your boys were the ones who came in here swinging. You and your boys are the ones who came in here asking for money that you didn't earn. And it's been you and your boys who tried to take this place apart right in front of me for no good reason."

"You don't know shit about our reasons. This don't concern you. That's why I'm giving you this one chance to back the fuck off before it does become your concern. Believe me, you don't want any part of that."

Rather than say another word, Clint kept his eyes fixed on Wade. Neither man budged until Clint shook his head so subtly that only Wade could see the movement.

That single motion was like a hammer smashing through a wall of ice. Suddenly, Wade stepped back and swung around to look at the men who'd gathered behind him.

"All right then," he said. "If this is how Mister Adams here wants it to go, then that's how it'll be. You know what you're supposed to do, boys. Let's get to it."

Clint didn't have to see the expression on Wade's face to know what signal was being given to the rest of his men. The Enforcers all looked like dogs who'd just been let loose and all of their hands started drifting too close to the guns at their sides.

Waiting until he saw Wade start to twist back around to face him, Clint stepped sideways in the same direction as Wade's turn. By matching the other man's motion, Clint managed to put himself completely out of the line of fire as Wade snatched the gun from his holster and brought it around to bear on the spot where his target had been.

Clint reached up and out with both hands. One hand took hold of Wade's arm just below the elbow and the other clamped down hard around Wade's wrist. In the space of the next split second, Clint could sense that Wade was about to take his shot. Praying that he would be fast enough, Clint tightened his grip even harder around the gray-haired man's wrist and twisted Wade's hand upward.

The gun roared once and kicked in Wade's fist. The blast was close enough to send a powerful ringing through both men's ears, but luckily the bullet sailed upward and dug into a rafter overhead. That shot, however, was like the start of a race as everyone inside the saloon started scrambling either for cover or a way out.

"Well, don't just stand there!" Red shouted to the men that had gathered around him. "Get in there and do your jobs!"

TWENTY-THREE

In the back of Clint's mind, he'd been hoping that the rest of Red's strong-arms were ready to back him up. He knew better than to count on them, however, since the only person a man could truly count on all of the time was himself. After all, Red's boys seemed like a good enough bunch but they had fallen into the habit of letting Wade run all over them.

Needless to say, when Clint heard Red sound the charge, it was a very welcome surprise. At least he didn't have to concern himself with every last one of the Enforcers. On the other hand, Clint figured Wade would keep him plenty busy all by himself.

On that account, Clint was absolutely right.

After firing his first round into the ceiling, Wade wasn't about to waste another shot. He was too experienced to panic like that and too determined to give up until he got that second chance. Rather than try to pull his wrist free of Clint's grasp just yet, he shifted his momentum to go in the way Clint was leading him. Once both men were moving in the same direction, Wade shifted his weight and snapped his arm outward with one strong motion.

The maneuver worked and no matter how strong he made his grip, Clint was unable to keep hold of Wade's arm. The gray-haired man had put all of his strength against Clint's thumb, which was the weakest link of any man's grip. As soon as he felt his hold fail, Clint started plotting several moves ahead. Such anticipation would be crucial if he was to control the situation without any by-standers getting hurt.

Clint pulled in both arms and took a quick, lunging step around Wade until he was behind the other man. From there, he stepped down with one leg behind Wade's knee, twisted his body around and extended his arm. All that remained for Clint to do was steel himself and use all his strength to twist his body back and swing his straight arm directly toward Wade's chest.

There was nothing too fancy about the move, but it served its purpose well enough. Clint's arm hit Wade like a wooden post and when Wade stumbled back, he tripped right over Clint's leg. The gray-haired man let out a vile curse as he fell over, but he still managed to keep himself from taking a shot without being centered on a target.

Behind Clint, the rest of Red's boys came running forward. Their steps hastened once they saw Wade taken down, but they still weren't ready for what was coming next. The Enforcers had their guns drawn and were squeezing their triggers while Red's boys had their sights set on a fistfight. Most of that first barrage, however, was more sound than fury and filled the air with lead hissing in a wide, disorganized pattern.

Glass was shattered and wood was splintered, but there wasn't much in the way of blood drawn. Several of Red's boys were clipped, but they were all grazing wounds at best. The initial shock of being fired at was enough to halt Red's charge and give the Enforcers a chance to mount an offensive of their own.

That was the difference between men who didn't mind

getting into a fight and those that liked fighting. The former could handle themselves when things got rough, but the latter were always ready to make things rougher. It was the difference between defending yourself and being out for blood.

That was the difference between Red's boys and the Enforcers. Unfortunately, it was a hell of a big difference.

Another round of gunfire erupted, but this time there were pained screams that followed. Clint couldn't exactly tell who'd been hit or how bad it was, but he knew one thing for sure and that was that things were about to get a whole lot worse. All he could do at the moment was try to keep Wade from playing too big a part in the fight. Hopefully by doing that, he could take some of the steam from the Enforcers as well.

Suddenly, Clint felt a dull pain flood his body from the chest down. The pain wasn't blinding, but it sapped a good portion of his momentum. The source of the pain was Wade's knee which had been slammed into Clint's solar plexus. He felt the wind fly out of him as though it were being sucked out by a set of bellows. Knowing that he could pull himself together if he just gave himself some time, Clint didn't give in to the weakness that threatened to take him over.

On the other hand, trying to work without any steam in his engine wasn't exactly the easiest thing to do either.

Every move Clint made was a struggle and just as he was getting a bit of momentum, Wade came along to pound it out of him.

A fist slammed solidly against Clint's back, landing just short of his kidneys. Even though the shot didn't land on target, it got close enough to send a jolt through Clint's system and turn his next few breaths into a labored wheeze.

Wade smirked when he saw that he'd done some damage and followed up with a chopping downward strike using the butt of his gun as a club. Before the chop could land, however, Wade was surprised to see Clint twist his upper body around and send a vicious backhand into the side of his leg.

Pain stabbed through Wade's leg, starting from where Clint's knuckles had landed and spread in all directions. His knee gave out for only a second, but that was enough to stagger the gray-haired man and give Clint a chance to catch his breath.

Seizing the chance he'd bought himself, Clint straightened up and sent a quick jab to Wade's chin. The moment he felt his fist land, Clint sent a stronger hook to knock Wade back and send a spray of blood through the air from a split lip.

Wade's expression was one of complete surprise. It seemed as though he had never been knocked around like that in all his years of fighting and that he could barely believe the blood that was flying was his own.

Clint spotted the gun in Wade's fist that was meant to smash into his own skull. Rather than allow that blow to land, Clint reached out with a lightning-quick hand and plucked the firearm from Wade's grasp. He knocked the handle into Wade's temple just hard enough to get the other man's attention and daze him a bit in the bargain.

"All right," Clint said as he took hold of the back of Wade's shirt as if he were grabbing a dog by the scruff of its neck. "Time for you to leave."

Still rattled from the knock to the head, Wade moved his feet to keep from being pulled off-balance, which carried him right where Clint wanted him to go. As the cobwebs started to clear, he found himself outside of The Lucky Lady and in the street.

Clint glanced over his shoulder and saw that Red's boys were holding their own once they'd closed the gap between themselves and the Enforcers. A few shots were still being fired, but Clint couldn't see any fatalities just yet. Most of the bystanders seemed to have found cover and a few of them were even starting to poke their heads out for a better look.

Seeing that, Clint figured he might as well give the customers something worth watching.

"Hey, Red," Clint shouted over his shoulder. "Tell your boys to start tossing these Enforcers out of here. They're no longer welcome."

Clint didn't see where Red was, but he could sure hear the saloon owner's voice when he replied, "Sure thing, Clint! You heard the man, boys! Let's clean house."

TWENTY-FOUR

Just as Clint had hoped, that little boast combined with seeing Wade himself get tossed out into the street was enough to fire up every one of Red's strong-arms. The brawlers stopped trying to out-fight the Enforcers and simply started grabbing hold of them and shoving them toward the door. In no time at all, Wade was joined by the rest of his men outside The Lady.

Clint had company as well. As each Enforcer was shown out the hard way, the man who'd done the showing stood next to Clint and prepared for whatever was to come next. Before too much longer, Clint and Wade stood facing each other like generals with their armies squaring off on opposing sides of a battlefield.

Clint couldn't help himself. "I guess you and your boys will just have to give that other saloon a try," he said with a shrug.

The barrel-chested guy on Red's payroll stepped up beside Clint and added, "Yeah. Let us know how their whiskey compares to ours."

Wade slowly shifted his glare from one side to another as he took stock of all the men gathered around him. After counting heads, he focused his stare back on Clint. Compared to the way he'd looked at Clint before, the expression on Wade's face this time was downright friendly.

"You made one hell of a mistake tonight, Adams," Wade snarled.

"Is that so? Seems like you didn't leave me much of a choice in the matter."

There was a moment as Wade became deathly quiet. As he wiped off some blood that was dripping from his lip, the gray-haired man took in a slow breath that seemed to suck out every bit of sound from the entire street. Every one of his men held their breaths, as did the men standing at Clint's side.

Although Clint felt the moment also, he didn't allow himself to be drawn into it as much as everyone else. It was a sheer contest of wills and the only combatants were Clint and Wade.

For a moment, Clint was certain the fight was going to be launched into a whole other level. Each of the Enforcers' eyes were twitching back and forth between Wade and the group standing in front of The Lucky Lady. Their fingers were itching to squeeze their triggers, but they didn't dare make that move until they got the go-ahead from Wade.

Although they hadn't started out brandishing their weapons, Red's boys had either done so already or were on the verge of clearing leather. Clint knew that all it would take was one jumpy soul to lose his patience and fire a shot. From there, everyone out there would fire their guns and Clint would be forced to follow suit.

So far, Red's boys were following their orders pretty well. It seemed to Clint that they weren't about to make another move until Clint made it first. The Enforcers were teetering on the precipice, but they seemed to be holding off equally well as they waited for the signal from Wade.

"Go on," Clint said in a stern voice. "Find somewhere else to drink and there won't be any more trouble."

Once he saw that Clint wasn't affected by the icy cold in his glare or the loaded silence in the air, Wade stepped back. That single movement was filled with a volume of meaning. "We'll see about that, Adams," he said after spitting a wad of blood onto the dirt. Turning to his men, Wade gave them a nod which prompted the Enforcers to holster their weapons.

As a group, Wade and his men turned their backs to The Lucky Lady and walked away.

Heavy footsteps clunked against the floorboards of the lobby and eventually rattled the planks outside The Lady's front door. Red came huffing outside, his face the color of a beet, as though he'd been the one to single-handedly eject the others.

"Holy shit," Red wheezed as he surveyed the scene outside his saloon. "I don't believe it. They're leaving." He turned to the closest of his men and asked, "Are they really leaving?"

The barrel-chested brawler who worked for Red turned to his boss, wearing a smile that practically covered his entire face. "They sure as hell are!"

With that, all of Red's boys let out a holler that echoed all the way down the street. Hearing that ruckus made Clint flinch. It was one thing to win a fight, but it was another thing to start bragging before the victory was completely assured. Sure enough, more than a couple of the Enforcers turned around and even made half a reach for their guns before being stopped by Wade. Clint might not have heard what Wade was telling his men, but he had a real good idea.

"Come on, Clint," Red said. "The next round's on me. Let's go back inside and enjoy it."

"Thanks, but I think I'll hold off on that for now," Clint replied. "There's still plenty more to do before we celebrate."

TWENTY-FIVE

It was only a matter of seconds after Red and his boys came back into The Lucky Lady that the rest of the saloon erupted with a similar round of cheers. Apparently, Red wasn't the only one in town who was waiting to see Wade get taken down a peg or two. It did Clint some good to see the smiles and feel the pats on the back, but he didn't let himself get swept up by it all.

He'd seen too many other early celebrations and had dealt with too many people like Wade. Also, there was the added unknown of Dutch Wilson. Clint wouldn't have a true feel for that man until he got a chance to look him square in the eyes. He'd gotten a good look into Wade's eyes, however, and Clint wasn't too happy with what he found.

Wade was a man that truly concerned him. He had kept his head throughout the entire fight and didn't make one move out of sheer rage. Most fighting men made mistakes because they rushed themselves or could be goaded into making a mistake by an opponent who kept his wits about him. A man as cold and calculating as Wade rarely made mistakes.

Clint recognized that fact because that was a trait that

had kept his own hide intact for so many years. It wasn't every day that Clint came across someone of his own caliber and though he couldn't say for certain if Wade was truly that good, he knew the gray-haired man deserved some respect.

For the moment, however, Clint decided to keep his reservations to himself. Looking around, he could feel the high spirits inside The Lucky Lady as though it was a perfumed scent that permeated the air. The folks in that saloon hadn't had a chance to celebrate like that in a long time. That much was obvious. If only half of what he'd heard was true, there hadn't been much reason to celebrate with someone like Wade coming around to tear off whatever pieces he wanted.

So Clint let the party go on and even let himself join in. He knew better than to let himself get drunk, but he couldn't say that he minded it when he felt the beer start to affect him as the music soared and the dancing girls kicked up their heels.

There were smiles all around and none of those smiles were wider than the ones being worn by Red and Bo. If Clint hadn't been on his guard, those two men alone would have bought him enough drinks to put a bull under a table. Every one of Red's boys came over to introduce themselves, but there was already so much noise in the room that Clint could barely understand a word that was said to him. So rather than try to memorize the list of names, he nodded and laughed at their jokes while tossing out a few of his own.

All in all, there was plenty of fun to be had amidst all that confusion. Compared to the time he'd spent at The Lighthouse, it was enough to make the entire city of San Francisco look tame. Compared to what he was normally used to in living quietly and sometimes out in the open country, it was enough to make Clint's head spin.

"We're starting up a poker game in the next room,"

Red told Clint as he staggered over and slapped him on the back. "I hear you're fairly good at cards."

Clint nodded and felt his gambler's instincts come to the surface the way a cat unsheathed its claws. "Yeah, I've played a hand or two."

"Then you should join us. It'll just be for me and my boys. There'll be plenty to drink and plenty of company if you get lonely," Red added with an overexaggerated wink.

"I think I'll let the rest have a shot at the women, but I've never turned my nose up at a good card game."

The truth of the matter was that Clint would have preferred some time to catch his breath. But since he was tired of being on his feet all day and made it a rule to never pay for a woman's company, he decided that a poker game was the best answer. Judging by the amount the others had been drinking, it could wind up being fairly profitable for Clint as well.

Just as Clint was about to follow Red into the next room where all the card tables were, his eye was diverted by a familiar sight. That blonde he'd seen before the most recent ruckus was again standing at the far end of the bar and she was also still looking straight at him. Her piercing gaze cut right through the beer in Clint's system and stoked up something deep inside of him like a match to dry kindling.

"Tell you what, Red," Clint said. "How about I join you in that game a little later?"

"What? All the boys'd like to—" Stopping when he saw where Clint's eyes were pointed, Red smiled broadly and gave him yet another slap on the shoulder. "Ahh. I get ya. We'll keep a seat open for you, but we won't hold our breaths."

"I appreciate the vote of confidence."

"Yeah, well just tell Victoria I send my best."

TWENTY-SIX

With his eyes focused on the blonde at the end of the bar, Clint barely took notice of the rest of the chaos filling the place. All the noises faded to a babble in the background and he barely even felt the occasional bumps from the people who didn't step aside for him.

She stood at the bar with one foot resting on the bottom rail and her elbow leaning against the polished wooden surface. Her hair flowed over her left shoulder, looking like spun gold in contrast to the black, lacy dress she wore. The dress hugged her body in a way that made her look regal and yet still showed off the impressive curves of her breasts and hips.

Soft, pink lips curled into a wide smile as Clint drew closer. When he was in arm's reach, she extended her hand and said, "Hello there. I'm surprised you noticed me in the middle of all this carrying-on."

Clint took her hand, which was soft to the touch, but displayed a definite strength in her grip. "I'm Clint Adams and I think I'd notice you even if the roof was falling down on top of me. You must be Victoria."

The look of surprise on the blonde's face was slight, but it was enough to put a little chink in her flawless veneer. Her smile became a little crooked and she lowered her head just a bit.

Before she could say anything else, Clint winked and explained, "Red sends his best."

Victoria nodded. "Then I take it you're the best?"

"Well now, that depends on who you ask."

"I don't have to ask anyone. All I need to do is watch the way you move." She let that hang in the air for a few moments before adding, "When things got rough, I mean. You moved like a man with a purpose."

"My purpose was to stay healthy."

Her eyes narrowed as she slowly shook her head. "No, I think there's more to it than that. You're a man who knows how to handle himself. If even a quarter of the things I've heard about you are true, then that's surely the case."

Clint's response to that had become reflexive after hearing those words so many times over the years. "You shouldn't believe everything you hear."

"That all depends on what I'm listening to." Leaning in a bit while keeping her eyes fixed on Clint's, she added, "But there are some things I'd definitely like to see for myself."

As they spoke, Clint couldn't help but notice the fact that the barkeep didn't once come over to her except to refill the glass of red wine she occasionally sipped from. That wasn't too odd in itself, until it was combined with the way everyone else at the bar gave her at least a foot or two of her own space.

Considering the beauty of her face and body as well as the sensuality of her every motion, that bit of space in a room filled with men was a downright miracle.

"I know this is sort of your party and all," she said in a soft voice that had no trouble reaching Clint's ears through the chaos. "But I was thinking we might go somewhere a little more quiet. Maybe somewhere we can be alone."

"That's funny. I was just thinking you seemed rather alone right here."

Victoria wasn't surprised by that comment at all. Instead, she merely took Clint's hand and led him even further toward the back of the room. "Come on," she said. "I know just the place. You'll even be back in time for your poker game."

She took him to what, at first, looked like nothing more than the back wall of the room. But laid perfectly in the grain of the wood, there was a door which blended seamlessly into the rest of the wall. The only thing to set it apart was the small, brass knob and the single word carved into the panel at eye level accented by gold paint that read, PRIVATE.

Turning the knob, Victoria entered a smaller room which was so well insulated from the rest of the saloon that most of the noise died away to a low thrum once she closed it off. The room itself was elegantly decorated and had a distinct femininity to the furnishings and textures. The walls and carpets were done up in dark reds that seemed to be made to match the wine that Victoria drank.

Chairs, two small tables and a modest desk were all made out of finely polished mahogany. Subdued paintings hung here and there and a small fireplace blazed at the wall adjacent to the door. And standing next to the fireplace, like another large piece of solid furniture, was one of the biggest men Clint had ever seen.

The guy had easily eight to ten inches of height over Clint and outweighed him by at least a hundred pounds. Judging by the way his arms and chest strained the fabric of his shirt, most of that weight was pure muscle. In fact, the man's arms were so massive that they almost completely hid the gun kept in the holster strapped around his shoulders.

When Clint and Victoria had entered the room, the hulking figure by the fireplace had barely moved. Even now that he'd been noticed, only his eyes shifted to track Clint's movements.

"Go on and enjoy the party, Solomon," Victoria said as she walked past the huge man. "Sounds like there's plenty out there to keep you busy for a while."

"Too bad he wasn't out there earlier," Clint said. "We sure could have used him."

Clint could see the bigger man's lip twitch in something that had to have been a repressed snarl. Victoria saw it too and stopped to run her hands along the outer edges of Solomon's arms.

"Red takes care of the saloon," she said in a way that didn't sound the least bit condescending. "And Solomon takes care of me." Turning to give Clint a little smile, she added, "Well, for the most part anyway."

When Solomon looked down at Victoria, it looked like a tree had just decided to uproot itself and speak. "You sure, ma'am?"

"I'm sure, Solomon. Mister Adams is working with us for the moment. We'd just like to have a little chat." When she placed her hand flat upon the huge man's shoulder, Victoria got him to lower himself down so she could whisper into his ear.

Solomon nodded approvingly while she spoke and straightened up once she was through. As he walked toward the door, Solomon's steps were surprisingly light. There was no way to keep them completely subdued, however, and Clint could feel the other man approaching him much the way natives could feel a train coming before the engine was even in sight.

Unpleasant possibilities came to Clint's mind when Solomon stopped directly in front of him and glowered down at him through eyes that were the same color as weathered tree bark. Clint found himself remaining still, the way he might if approached by a prowling wolf.

Slowly, Solomon's arm reached out and his hand unfurled. "Nice to meet you, Mister Adams."

Relieved, Clint nodded and shook the other man's hand. Unlike most big fellas, Solomon didn't feel the need to impress his physical advantage and kept his grip firm, yet manageable.

"Same here, Solomon," Clint replied. "If you're any good at poker, you can keep my seat warm at Red's table."

"I may just do that. But whatever I win," he added, giving his voice a mean edge, "I keep."

"You got it."

With that, Solomon walked out the door and shut it behind himself. Suddenly, it seemed as though one of the walls of the room just got up and left.

"He's a good man," Victoria said. "But I'm glad to have you all to myself."

TWENTY-SEVEN

Victoria was so comfortable in her surroundings that she seemed to drift around the room. The carpet beneath her feet absorbed the sound of her footsteps, making it feel as though they were someplace sacred. Clint had to remind himself several times that he was still in the same saloon that was erupting with a huge celebration at that very moment. Thinking that it was the same place that had been alive with a huge brawl felt damn close to impossible.

Standing beside the small table with the glasses and wine bottle, Victoria poured some of the wine into an empty glass before refilling her own. She then turned toward Clint and held out the new glass for him.

"This is a fancy place you've got here," Clint said as he accepted the glass from Victoria's hand. "I first thought this might have been Red's office, but that doesn't seem to fit."

"No, this isn't Red's. It's the one room in this whole building that I call my own. Hardly anyone ever comes back here." Glancing around at the walls and soaking up the subdued light coming from several lit candles, she added, "I like to think it's my own little secret."

"I hope you don't mind me asking, but why does Red let you have this space all to yourself? Does he also pay Solomon's wages?"

"Actually, me having this little place of my own was part of the deal when Red and I built The Lucky Lady."

"Really? I didn't know he had another partner."

"Well, I like to keep silent about it. I'm not about to hide what I do, but it seems to make things go smoother when everyone thinks there's a man in charge." Although there was some bit of distaste when she said that, Victoria didn't seem bitter.

"How far back do you and Red go?" Clint asked.

She had to think about that for a second. Putting the glass to her lips, Victoria took a slow sip and let the rim stay in contact with her mouth as the tip of her tongue brushed over the wet surfaces. Lowering the glass just a bit, she swallowed the bit of wine she'd taken in and said, "It's been about eleven years that Red and I have been in business together."

"And it's just been business?"

"Yes, Clint. Only business."

"Just checking," Clint said as he gently tapped his glass against Victoria's and placed his other hand upon her hip. "I'd hate to step on anyone's toes."

"Don't worry about that." Victoria's mouth was so close to Clint's that he could feel the warmth of her breath. Her body was giving off its own heat as well, which became apparent when she pressed up against him. "I just hope you don't mind being brought all the way over here from San Francisco. I hear you were having a hell of a time over there."

"I was, but everything comes to an end."

"It was my idea to contact you."

"Is that so?"

Nodding, Victoria set her glass down onto the table before taking Clint's glass and placing it on the table as well. "I mentioned it to Red in passing, but I knew he'd want to bring you here. We may be partners, but he likes to think he's the man in charge more often than not."

Victoria's voice was like a soft, velvety purr that sent a subtle shiver through Clint's body. Unlike younger women who relied on their bodies alone, Victoria appeared to be in her late thirties and knew a man's desires almost as well as she knew her own. She was also very comfortable with herself. After all, she had every reason to be confident since her curves were firm and well-maintained. Her hands were soft, strong and unashamed as they easily found their way from one spot to the next.

Clint was enjoying the slow, erotic dance they were doing. As much as he wanted to throw her down and get her out of her clothes, he held back. What made the effort both more difficult and more rewarding was the knowledge that she might just throw him down at any second herself.

"So when you wanted to contact me," Clint said, "what exactly did you have in mind?"

Victoria's hips ground slowly back and forth. Every so often, she would push them forward so she could brush against the growing bulge between Clint's legs. "I wanted you to help clean out the trash in this place. We needed something more than just another hired hand and when I heard you were already in San Francisco, I thought it was meant to be."

"So that's all there was to it?"

Pressing against him a little harder, Victoria rubbed her breasts against Clint's chest and ground against his erection even more. "I also wanted you to get away from Karl Patrice. He uses people up like they were cattle. A good man won't get what he's worth working for someone like that."

"Very thoughtful of you."

"Also, I wanted you to . . ." She stopped when Clint

wrapped his arms around her and pushed his hips against her so she could feel the full extent of the effect she had upon him.

When he moved, she moved with him as if their bodies were already joined. Clint's hands slipped around hers, guiding her away from the table in slow, grinding steps. She kept her eyes locked on his, allowing herself to be led wherever he wanted to take her.

Victoria's breath caught in her throat as her shoulders bumped against a wall. Even the texture of that was soft and when she was pressed against it, she could feel the rumble of all the people moving inside the saloon and could hear the dull roar of all the noise outside that room. Clint's body was strong and muscular against hers, blocking her from moving away. Even though she was right where she wanted to be, Victoria felt the flush of excitement knowing that he wasn't about to let her get away.

"I wanted you to . . ." Once again, she was cut off. This time, her breath was taken away by the feel of Clint's hand sliding up her body to cup her breast over her dress. The motion of her hips caused her legs to open just enough for him to push forward with his hips and grind his erection against the hot spot between her thighs.

The touch of him felt primal and so powerfully erotic that Victoria wanted nothing more than to let him feel the warm dampness that waited for him beneath her skirts. When she caught her breath, she arched her back and whispered, "I just wanted you."

TWENTY-EIGHT

"God *damn* that Red! God damn him and that fucking bitch whore he keeps to make all his decisions for him!" When he spoke those words, the slender man with the thinning silver hair slammed his fist on the top of an over-sized desk to accentuate each and every curse.

The man who did the cursing was slightly below average height, but carried himself as though he towered above everyone else in the room. His frame was leaning toward the bony side, but sported enough muscle to keep him looking trim and athletic. Deep lines creased his face, which became even deeper as he scowled at the others standing in front of him.

At the front of that group was Wade and Lowell. The latter kept his hat in hand while the former stood as if he was merely waiting for the storm to pass so he could get a word in edgewise.

"Did you get to her at least?" the man behind the desk asked. "Did you at least get far enough into that shit hole of a saloon to get a look into that blond whore's eyes?"

Lowell opened his mouth as though he meant to answer, but thought twice before uttering a word. Instead of saying what was on his mind, he looked over to Wade with a not-too-subtle pleading in his eyes.

Seeing the other man's panic combined with the way his mouth hung open like a bass gaping for water, Wade had to fight back the impulse to haul off and knock Lowell out right then and there. The look in his eyes must have said plenty, because Wade didn't have to lift a finger before Lowell was shutting his mouth and backing up a step.

"Well?" the man behind the desk said as he switched his gaze between the two men.

"Don't act so surprised, Dutch," Wade said with exasperation. "I told you way back when that Red was sending someone out to get in touch with Clint Adams. I even told you when Bo was coming back and bringing Adams with him."

Although Dutch listened, he didn't seem any calmer. In fact, he just seemed to have a single target to aim all the steam that was building up inside of him. "You sure did. And what the hell do you want from me? A medal for doing what I pay you to do?"

"What I'm saying is—"

"What you're saying isn't what I wanted to hear. It's not even what I asked you!"

Normally, Wade would never have put up with someone talking to him that way. Even though Dutch paid his salary, that didn't give him the right to browbeat someone used to blazing his own trails. On the other hand, Wade had never been paid the amount of money that Dutch paid to keep him on.

That kind of money went a long way. That was good, because Wade had to dig deep to keep himself from blasting a hole straight through Dutch's face. Rather than indulge that particular desire, Wade took a deep breath and nodded.

"I told you go in there and bust that place up, didn't I?" Dutch asked.

Wade nodded.

"But that wasn't all, was it? I wanted you to go into that place, call out both of the owners. Both of them! And when you did that, I wanted you to make them watch while you took that saloon apart. Do you remember me asking you to do that?"

"I went in to—" Wade started, but he was cut off by the piercing bark of Dutch's angered voice.

"That wasn't my question, Wade! Do you remember what I told you going in?"

Wade's breath came out of him like steam through a piston. Nodding once, he could feel the heat rising in his face as he said, "Yeah. I remember."

"And is that what happened?"

"No."

This time, when Dutch's hands came down on top of his desk, they were flat and only hit with a fraction of the force that he'd been using before. "There now. That's better. Doesn't it feel better to go along with me instead of fighting every step of the way?"

But Wade couldn't get himself to nod and play along any longer. He kept from saying what he wanted and from doing what he wanted, but he'd be damned if he was going to stroke the other man like some spoiled puppy. There wasn't enough money in the world to pay for that kind of service.

Dutch was too busy wallowing in his own moment, however. Knowing Wade as well as he did, the man behind the desk knew how far he'd pushed and considered it a victory in itself. "So tell me. Is it really Clint Adams, or is it just some gunslinger Red hired to try and impress everyone?"

"It's Adams," Wade answered.

"How can you tell? Have you met the man before?"

"I saw the way he handled himself in that fight. He wasn't just some hired gun. There was more to him than that."

"What're you talking about?"

"I looked into his eyes," Wade said simply. "He said he was Clint Adams and from what I saw, I got no reason to think he was lying."

Dutch considered that for a moment before nodding once and getting up from his chair. Walking around his desk, he reached out and slapped Wade on the back as though he'd just sold the other man some property. "Well, if that's good enough for you, then it's good enough for me!" Dutch said with almost as much enthusiasm as he'd had when he was screaming for damnation.

Dutch's eyes fixed on the rest of the Enforcers while keeping his hand draped over Wade's shoulder. "That leaves only two more matters to resolve. First of all, we need to deal with Adams so we can finish our business with Red and that blond bitch. But that one's been around for a while. The other matter is more pressing. I need someone to pay for what happened tonight."

"I think I should—" Lowell started to say.

"You think you should step up and speak for the rest of your Enforcers?" Dutch finished. "That's very upstanding."

Although he looked surprised by the words that had been put into his mouth, Lowell nodded and agreed with them nonetheless. "Thanks."

Without another word, Dutch took his hand off Wade's shoulder, balled it into a fist and drove it so far into Lowell's gut that his knuckles damn near snapped the other man's spine. Dutch didn't waste a moment and as soon as Lowell was bent over from the pain of the sudden attack, there was another one on its way.

Dutch sent a straight jab into the other man's face, followed by a savage uppercut that had all of his previous anger behind it. His fist slammed into Lowell's chin, crunching the bone and knocking his jaw to an awkwardly skewed angle. From there, Dutch clasped one fist around another and swung them into the other side of Lowell's face as though he were swinging a club.

That impact sent Lowell to the floor and none of the other men in the room dared to go to his aid. Dutch stood over him and looked down as though he was about to spit. Instead, he pulled his leg back and delivered a kick straight into Lowell's groin.

Balled up on the floor, Lowell let out an agonized wheeze and spat up a mixture of blood and vomit.

"Get this spineless cocksucker out of my sight," Dutch said. "And the next time I see Red or that bitch partner of his, I want them to look twice as bad as that."

Wade was the first one to help scoop Lowell off the ground and soon the other Enforcers were pitching in.

Dutch had already gone back behind his desk and was studying a leather-bound ledger listing various sums of money and projected profit margins.

TWENTY-NINE

Victoria and Clint stayed so close that their bodies were touching in every spot they possibly could. Even as they started feeling for the edges of the other's clothes, they managed to keep in contact as much as possible. This wasn't a conscious effort, but more of an attraction that was so strong there was nothing they could do to fight it.

Being a woman who knew what she wanted and was not afraid to go after it, Victoria pulled open Clint's shirt and immediately went on to work on loosening his pants. She only paused every now and then to let out an anxious moan when Clint made progress in peeling the clothes off her body.

"Is this why you brought me here?" Clint asked as his hand slipped through the slit in Victoria's dress to feel the bare skin of her thigh.

Letting out a breath and tugging down Clint's jeans, she replied, "To Crystall? No. To this room? Yes. Actually," she added as her hand slipped into Clint's jeans to wrap around his cock where she could start stroking it up and down, "this is why I brought you in here. I wanted to feel you for myself."

Clint closed his eyes and leaned his head back so he

could savor the feel of Victoria's hand working on him. Her touch was perfect; strong, yet also gentle right when she needed to be. Although he could have stood there and let her stroke him all night long, Clint had other plans.

Opening his eyes, he once again took hold of Victoria's hands and pressed them against the wall. She let herself hit the wall and let out a breathy moan as she did. Once Clint lifted her arms up so the backs of her hands were against the wall and over her head, he moved his own hands down to her elbows and then shoulders.

Victoria kept her hands right where Clint had put them. Now it was her turn to close her eyes, lean back and enjoy what was being done to her. She writhed slowly as Clint moved his hands over her breasts and then down to her heaving stomach. Suddenly, his hands jumped back up to cup her large breasts, squeezing them firmly before roughly pulling away the upper part of her dress.

The material came away easily and Clint almost ripped it in his haste to get Victoria undressed. Her breasts were slightly bigger than what he could hold in his hands and they were capped with large, dark nipples. Those nipples became instantly erect when Clint moved his mouth down to brush against them one at a time, his tongue flicking out to send even more shivers throughout her entire body.

As he licked her nipples and ran his tongue between her breasts, Clint kept sliding Victoria's dress down until it passed over her hips. From there, the garment dropped to the floor. Clint's hands were below her waist already so it was only a matter of inches before he could cup her generous buttocks and massage the smooth skin.

Victoria was moaning now and her eyes were open to show the primal longing she felt for him. She was just as rough with his clothes as Clint was to hers when she stripped him out of his shirt and jeans in the space of a few pounding heartbeats.

Sliding one hand over the back of Victoria's thigh,

Clint felt her anticipate his desire and lift that leg to wrap around his waist. Her hand came down to guide the tip of his cock between the wet lips of her pussy. From there, all he had to do was push forward to bury his penis completely inside of her.

Both of them let out moans of relief and pleasure as their longing was finally sated. Clint pumped in and out of her in a steady rhythm as Victoria worked her hips back and forth to make each stroke feel that much better.

Clint watched the changes in her face as he moved inside of her, letting his eyes occasionally wander down to her breasts which swayed and jiggled as the two of their bodies moved. Victoria's stomach was a gentle slope leading down to the patch of fine, blond hair between her legs. When he looked up again, he caught Victoria studying his body in much the same way, her eyes lingering on the shaft of his cock as it glided in and out of her pussy.

At that moment, Clint was overtaken by another urge and let himself follow it through almost immediately. Stepping back from her, he put both hands upon her hips so he could lead her away from the wall and toward the back of the room. He then spun her around, sending Victoria's body in a tight semi-circle and her hair flying out like a skirt around a dancer's waist.

Her eyes lit up when she saw what he was after and took a few quick steps toward what Clint had pointed her toward. When she was there, she bent at the waist and put both her hands flat upon the edge of her desk. Victoria arched her back and pushed her backside out toward Clint while slowly turning to look at him over her shoulder.

Clint was right behind her, drinking in the sight of her naked body displayed so perfectly in front of him. The slope of her spine was a gentle line that flowed down to the inviting curve of her buttocks. When he ran his fingers along that same line, he felt the shiver run through Victoria's body. As he stepped forward a little more and moved his fingers between her thighs, Clint felt her move her legs apart and lower her shoulders in anticipation of what was about to come.

Centering himself just right, Clint felt his erection become so hard that it almost started to hurt. Even though the wait had been less than a minute, he felt like it had been hours since he'd been inside of her. The only thing he knew at that moment was that he couldn't wait one more second before placing his cock between her legs, taking hold of Victoria's hips and thrusting all the way inside.

Every time he pumped into her, Clint could see the muscles in Victoria's back tensing. He could feel other muscles tensing as well, squeezing his shaft as though she didn't want to let him go. As he continued to thrust in and out, Clint massaged her hips until her powerful moans became a contented purr.

Suddenly, Victoria gripped onto the edge of the desk as she whipped her hair back over her shoulders. A powerful orgasm was creeping up on her. Even Clint could feel it in the way her breathing changed and her body braced for the impact.

As she began to climax, Victoria's vagina squeezed tightly around him, bringing Clint to his own apex. As the pleasure coursed through her, Victoria's head bowed and she held onto the desk as her legs started to get weak.

Seconds later, Clint was taken to the edge and pushed immediately over it. The sensation of her body and the sight of her naked skin spread out before him was enough to drive any man insane with pleasure. There was no holding it back and Clint didn't even think of trying.

For a few seconds, they were both in the grips of their orgasms. In that moment, the room became quiet as they both held their breath and let the intense sensations work their way through their flesh. Clint was the first to open his eyes and soon after, Victoria lazily swung her head around to look at him. There was a subtle look of disappointment on her face when he disengaged from her, but that only lasted until she turned around and sat facing him on the edge of her desk.

"Something tells me you're used to having women throw themselves at you," she said with a mischievous grin.

"And something tells me you're used to having whatever you set your sights on."

Nodding, Victoria let her eyes wander down along Clint's naked front. "Just because I'm a woman doesn't mean I can't reach out and take what I want," she said, reaching out and taking hold of his penis so she could stroke it between both hands. "Sometimes, I allow myself to be more forward than others."

"I'm glad to be one of those times," Clint said with a smile of his own.

Still stroking his cock, she rubbed it until his erection returned in full force. Spreading her legs open, she rubbed his tip against her moist lips and whispered, "Who said there's just going to be one time?"

THIRTY

The festivities went on throughout the entire night and well into the next morning. That included the festivities that were held in the public areas of The Lucky Lady as well as those being held in private. By the time the sun came up the next morning, it would have been hard to find a single person who wasn't still feeling the effects of the night before.

Red and most of his boys were in the dining room sipping from whatever concoctions they used to ease the slamming pains put there from drinking too much liquor. The cleaning staff were still picking up reminders from the bash and the people still in their beds meant to stay there for several more hours.

There were some, however, who weren't inclined to sit back and merely gather their strength. There were still plenty around who meant to use that strength to their advantage before another hour slipped through their fingers.

Although he'd spent the night in the room given to him upstairs in The Lucky Lady, Clint felt as though he hadn't even seen the inside of it. Having returned to that room at some ungodly hour after using every available surface in Victoria's office for their own pleasure, it seemed to Clint as though he could scarcely even recall what his own room looked like.

He was one of the few to get up early, even though his body cried out for a few more hours of sleep. After a quick breakfast and a few words with some of the young brawlers on Red's payroll, Clint spotted a familiar giant lurking in the back of the room just waiting to be spotted. Although it was impossible to miss Solomon standing there, most of the others seemed used to ignoring him. Either that, or they were too intimidated by the hulking figure to meet his gaze.

Clint would have had no trouble believing either explanation. For his own part, however, he wasn't in the habit of ignoring much of anything. All too often, it was the little details that made the difference in tight situations. As soon as he spotted Solomon, Clint gave the big man a nod. Solomon returned the greeting and motioned for Clint to come over to where he was standing.

"Excuse me, gentlemen," Clint said as he got up from where he sat with Red's ailing crew. "Looks like I'm being summoned."

"Aw, you should tell whoever it is to—" The muscular young man stopped what he was saying the moment he turned to get a look at who was doing the summoning. After flashing Solomon an uncomfortable smile, the guy turned back to his tomato juice and toast and pretended as though he hadn't just lost all the color in his face.

Clint found it funny at how everyone tiptoed around Solomon. Since the production of the Peacemaker, a man's physical size didn't amount to much anymore. Then again, there would always be that instinctual reflex to bow your head to the dominant member of the pack. Apparently, Solomon was that member and Clint was more than happy to be on the huge man's good side.

"Good morning, Sol," Clint said as he walked up to the hulking figure. "You mind if I call you Sol?"

Suddenly, the giant recoiled a bit and furrowed his brow. "No," he said after a moment or two. "I don't mind."

Clint could tell right off that Solomon probably hadn't been treated in such a friendly manner by anyone but Victoria for some time. That was a shame, because the big man's entire manner changed after that one, simple question.

"You look better than most of the rest in here," Clint said in a slightly lowered voice. "After last night's party, I'm surprised so many of them are able to keep their heads up."

Solomon looked down at Clint and laughed once to himself. "After last night, I'm surprised you're even able to walk straight."

Now, it was Clint's turn to change color. He wasn't the type to embarrass easily, but that comment had simply blindsided him to the point that his cheeks immediately started to flush. "Now that's a fine way to talk to a man who gave up a premium seat at an exclusive card game."

"That room's filled with card games," Solomon replied dryly. "That's what it's for." After a moment of maintaining his stony facade, the big man let his friendly smile return. "I did make out pretty well last night."

"I thought you would. Those boys were drunk, ready to play and didn't want to think about what they lost until later on. All they needed was someone to come along and pluck the money from their pockets."

"Yeah, well I would've gotten more if I didn't have to keep answering questions about what all the noise was that came from Miss Lauren's office."

"All right, all right. Just take me to where you wanted me to go."

Solomon chuckled under his breath and led the way.

THIRTY-ONE

When Clint was shown into Victoria's office, he almost didn't recognize the place. Nothing had been changed to the room itself, but there was the addition of enough others inside the place to make it feel almost as crowded as the rest of the saloon did the night before. At that moment, Clint realized just how small the office truly was now that he and Victoria didn't have the entire space to themselves.

Sitting in one of the larger chairs in front of the desk was Red who only stopped what he was saying long enough to see who'd entered the room. There were only a few other chairs about and those were filled with older men who looked to be business types just going by the look of their suits and perfectly trimmed hair and whiskers.

That only left one other seat in the office, which was the one behind the modest desk. Victoria sat there in a way that left no question that she was the one in charge. At least, that was the way it was inside that room and she carried that mantle perfectly. She sat listening as Red thundered on about the state of affairs and all the businessmen looked on. She kept her arms in her lap and her fingers loosely entwined. Acknowledging Clint with a

127

friendly glance, she nodded toward the space where she
wanted him to wait.

What little space there was inside the room was immediately taken away when Solomon stepped inside and
shut the door behind him. In that instant, the room seemed
to get that much more cramped and the air became that
much thicker in Clint's lungs.

"We're nowhere close to where we were a week ago,"
Red said in a voice that was just a little too loud for his
surroundings. "Once we get Dutch and his people out of
here for good, they won't have much else to hang on to
and they'll probably just move on to some other town.
They might leave for different parts of the globe. Who
gives a shit, so long as they leave?"

Victoria took a breath, pausing before saying exactly
what she was thinking. "Isn't that jumping the gun just a
little?"

Before Red could respond, he was cut off by the businessman sitting to his left. "I agree. While things have
taken a turn for the better thanks to Mister Adams, I don't
know if we should abandon our other plan just yet."

"I've got a problem with that plan, Harrold. I always
did and you know it."

"That doesn't take away from any of its value."

"That is if there was even anything of value in there
to begin with."

If the room had been filled with men wearing guns or
even men more physically intimidating, Clint might have
worried about a punch being thrown. As it was, the worst
the older men had to offer was intent stares and uncomfortable silence. Still, there was no mistaking the fact that
plenty was brewing beneath the surface.

Obviously not affected by the discomfort either, Victoria gave the men a few moments to stare each other
down before stepping in once again. "Right now, let's just
try to work with the plan that we've already started. Clint

is right here," she said, motioning toward him with an open hand, "and he's been working out just fine."

A few of the businessmen glanced back at him, but not all. The ones who did look his way regarded him much as they would a gun hanging on a rack. Suddenly, Clint knew how Solomon must feel standing right along with the rest of the heavy furniture.

"Clint's been doing a hell of a job," Red told the others. "Anyone who was in earshot of this place last night would know that for themselves."

Looking at Red with the same amount of measured patience that she'd shown to the businessmen, Victoria nodded and said, "And since he's working out, we should see where that leads. As for the other plan, we'll just keep that in mind should this one fail. How does that sound?"

She looked around at the faces gathered in front of her desk and regarded each one in turn, without paying any one of them any extra attention. She didn't get much of a response from the men, but she apparently saw enough to satisfy her for the time being.

Standing up and placing both hands on her desk, Victoria said, "All right, then. It sounds like we're done for the moment. Does anyone else have anything to say?"

It was obvious from the tone in her voice that Victoria didn't want to hear another word from any of the men. None of those men seemed too anxious to go against that, so they each got up and went through the short process of saying their good-byes. Victoria shook each of the businessmen's hands and gave them all a warm smile before they left.

Red stayed behind, but only for a moment. "They're chomping at the bit," he said to Victoria. "I can feel it. I swear, if they so much as—"

"They won't," she said, interrupting him as gently as possible. "And I'm sure we'll hear something from someone if they start moving in that direction. Clint here has bought us some time, so just sit back and enjoy some of it. You look like you barely even got any sleep."

A smile came onto Red's face that pushed away the concern that had been there only moments before. "Yeah, I did raise some hell last night. I doubt if I slept for more than half an hour or so."

"I was kept pretty busy myself," she said, giving Clint a quick, meaningful look. "Make sure at least half the boys are seeing straight before getting some rest. I doubt we'll have much trouble right away."

"Yeah, you're probably right." Red shot a quick glance over to Clint and wasn't quite successful in holding back a smirk. "I guess I'll leave you two alone for a bit. Clint, come and see me after you're through in here."

As he walked by Clint, Red gave him a chuck on the shoulder and left the office. Solomon stepped aside to let Red pass, but didn't leave the office once the other man had gone. Instead, he clasped his hands in front of him and took up his normal, motionless position by the door.

All Clint had to do was look into Victoria's eyes to know that this visit wasn't going to be half as pleasant as the last time he'd been inside that same room.

"There's going to be trouble," she said plainly.

Sometimes Clint hated being right.

THIRTY-TWO

Clint took a seat that had been occupied by one of the businessmen only a minute or two before. "Trouble?" he asked. "What kind of trouble?"

"Those men that were in here were part of the local business committee run by shop and saloon owners in the area. We meet every week to discus the state of affairs so we can all profit as a town instead of competing against each other for profits."

"Sounds like a smart way to operate."

"I thought so," Victoria said. "It was my idea."

"Is that how you and Red got together to run this place?"

"No, we met a little while before that. He was playing faro in Sacramento and I was working the room."

"What kind of work are we talking about?"

"Let's just say I was experienced in separating men from their money. Anyway, Red was drunk and put everything he had into three last plays. He asked me to pick where to place his bets, I did and he won enough money to open his own place."

"So you're not just his partner."

"That's right. I'm The Lucky Lady. And ever since

then, he's trusted my judgment on a good many things. Unfortunately, not all the men in this community are so open to another opinion besides their own. Especially," she added, "if that other person is a woman."

"Those men in here seemed to accept you as one of their own."

"On the face of things, maybe. But when it comes down to the big decisions, they tend to falter. That's where that trouble I mentioned comes in." Victoria reached into one of the drawers of her desk and removed a flat metal case. Opening the case, she pulled out one cigarette and offered the case to Clint.

He declined.

After putting the cigarette between her lips, she struck a match and touched the flame to the end of the cigarette. Her lips pursed together in a soft, pink pucker so she could blow out the flame. Either the simple move was intended to entice Clint or it was so practiced that she didn't even realize how subtly erotic it was.

Whichever it was, that little puff of air from her pursed lips did indeed send a chill beneath Clint's skin.

"I thought they'd be happy now that you're here," she said while flicking the spent match into a glass ashtray. "Unfortunately, they're not as happy with your progress as I'd anticipated."

"Jesus Christ, I haven't even been here that long and I did well enough to merit a party last night. What else were they expecting?"

"I don't mean to offend you, but—"

"You're not the one offending me," Clint interrupted. "That is, unless you're just saying this to light a fire under me."

Victoria laughed once, but more at the statement rather than the man who'd made it. "Trust me, Clint. I don't see any reason to light a fire under you. If that was the case, I wouldn't have kept you so busy last night. Truth be told,

I thought you did a hell of a job and I felt like celebrating myself."

Watching her speak, Clint looked for any of the telltale signs that she was lying. Having spent years playing poker, Clint had picked up so many of those signs from so many people that he couldn't even list them all if he'd wanted to. What it all boiled down to was a well-honed instinct rather than just some mental list.

For the moment, that instinct told Clint that he wasn't being lied to. Actually, he hadn't had that suspicion at any time since he'd talked to Victoria. And as for her wanting to get him riled up for one reason or another, she was too good at getting her way with men to make such a major error in judgment.

"All right then," Clint said once he felt his blood stop boiling. "What was their problem then?"

Victoria took one puff from her cigarette and put it down in the ashtray. "To put it simply, they had their own notion about what to do regarding Dutch and his men. To be fair, those other businesses have been around longer than this saloon and they've been paying Dutch's protection for many more years than Red and I. The only reason I bring that up is because it makes it easier to understand why those others might be more impatient or even more, for lack of a better word, desperate."

Clint's instincts kicked in again. This time, they told him he might not like the answer to his next question. "What did they have in mind?"

"They wanted to hire some men of their own. Except, the men they had in mind aren't exactly of your caliber. They're more of the work-for-hire types."

"You mean hired guns."

"Well, hired killers would be more like it. And not only were the rest of the committee behind that idea, but they already had their group picked out."

"Did they mention any names?" Clint asked, already dreading the response he might get.

"Yes," Victoria responded, tapping her bottom lip as she sifted through her thoughts. Snapping her fingers, she nodded and said, "Yes, I remember now. It was Nick Ironside . . . I think."

Clint let out the breath he'd been holding and sank back into his chair. "You mean Nick Ironhorse?"

Shrugging, she said, "That was it. I take it you've heard of him?"

"Yeah. I've heard of him and your committee couldn't have made a worse choice."

"They seemed to think this person was good at his job. They even brought him in to discuss what he might do to earn his pay and I got the impression that he was the type of man they had in mind. In my former line of work, I got pretty good at spotting those dangerous types. Too many girls without that skill turned up dead or just didn't turn up at all."

"Oh, Nick's a fine killer. I meant the choice was bad if your committee wanted to save this town. At least Dutch's violence is contained. Setting Nick loose is like breaking a dam to put out a campfire."

THIRTY-THREE

So far, Victoria had been very good at maintaining her composure. Of course, she'd let that slip when it had been just her and Clint alone in the office, but that was a different situation entirely. When dealing with Red or that committee, she'd made it perfectly clear that she was a force to be reckoned with, if not the force driving everyone else.

When she heard Clint talk about Nick Ironhorse, on the other hand, she was unable to keep herself from slipping just a bit. Her mouth didn't exactly fall open, but her expression slipped just enough for Clint to notice. If he was sitting across from her at a card table, Clint would know for certain that she'd missed whatever hand she was pulling for.

"Have you met this person?" Victoria asked, pulling herself together and repairing her facade.

Clint shook his head. "Not really. I've crossed paths with some of the men that ride with him and they were a rough enough bunch in their own regard. As for Nick himself, I've seen his handiwork and have heard enough about him to put a good picture together for myself."

"And just how bad is that picture, Clint? I need to

know since you're the only one I think I can trust here."

"For starters, do you know how Nick got his name?"

"His name?" she asked. "Which name?"

"Ironhorse. That's not his real name."

"I didn't know that."

Clint leaned forward so he could stare directly into Victoria's eyes. "The Navajo gave him that name when he was hired on by the Army to clear out some of their problem areas for local settlers. They were offering cash for scalps and Nick had no problem signing on.

"You see, the way he worked was simple. He'd ask around, maybe do a bit of half-assed tracking until he found someone with dark skin. Nick and whoever was with him would kill whoever they found and let the quartermaster sort them out." Clint scowled at the foul taste his own words had in his mouth. "Blacks, Mexicans, some were just dark skinned. All of them were killed and Nick didn't give a rat's ass so long as he got his money.

"Once he got wind of a group of Navajo heading south, Nick latched onto them like a dog sinking its teeth into fresh meat. He'd follow the travelers, attack them and let just enough survive to lead him to the next batch. Nick took out a few little camps and a village that way because he recruited more killers as he went along."

"Oh my God," Victoria said as she covered her mouth with her hand. "Are you sure about this?"

Clint nodded solemnly. "That much spilled blood doesn't go unnoticed. I heard about this from both sides of the story, Army and the Navajo. Both accounts differed in some way, but Nick came out pretty much the same."

"Good Lord."

"Toward the end of that run," Clint continued, "the Navajo gave Nick the name of Ironhorse because they said trying to stop him was like trying to stop the white man from laying down their tracks. Like it or not, the iron horse just rolls right through."

Clint leaned back into his chair and let his words sink in. Victoria didn't even try to hide the revulsion she was feeling at that moment. Her hand seemed unable to drop down from where it still covered her mouth.

"Could there be some mistake?" she asked.

"I doubt it. Even among other killers, that's not exactly the type of reputation a man wants to own up to. Besides that, Nick's got a price on his head big enough to buy out your friend Patrice's place in San Francisco. Someone would be insane to pretend to be Nick Ironhorse."

"Well, maybe this other person is pretending," Victoria offered hopefully. "I mean, wouldn't the real man change his name or try to hide with a bounty that big out for him?"

"That's true. Have you seen the man your committee wants to hire?"

"In passing, yes. They knew I was against hiring him, so they met with him behind my back."

"Was he about my height, dark hair, thin build with bad skin?"

Victoria's head sank down as though someone had cut the string holding her up. "Yes."

"That sounds like him to me."

"But I thought you never really got a good look at him."

"I haven't," Clint answered. "I just described the picture off his wanted poster."

"Good Lord," she said. "What have they done?"

"I'll tell you what they've done, Victoria. That committee has hired on one of the most bloodthirsty killers I've ever heard of. Speaking from experience, I know how stories about a man can get out of hand. But if even half of the ones about Nick Ironhorse are true, I'd say you've got one hell of a problem on your hands. Is there any way you can talk the others out of bringing him here?"

Victoria took a deep breath to steady her nerves before

getting up and walking over to the table where she kept her wineglasses and bottle. Pouring herself a glass, she drank half of it down in one hearty sip. With her nerves steadied somewhat, she turned to Clint and said, "That's what today's little meeting was about."

"And what would you have me do instead?" Clint asked. "I doubt those businessmen would listen to much of what I had to say."

"I was thinking you might pay Dutch a visit. You know, maybe talk to him and see if you can get some bigger results by going straight to the source."

"You mean see if I can intimidate him."

Victoria shrugged, but didn't deny the statement. "You and I both know it won't be long before Wade comes back here with more Enforcers along with him."

"So what exactly is that committee's problem with me anyway? Surely it's not something that my chatting with Dutch will fix."

"I guess even after all you've done, they think Ironhorse could do more."

"Well, if they want someone to come into town and kill Dutch, his men, his family and anyone else who gets in the way then, yeah, Ironhorse will do a whole lot more than I will. The only problem you'll have is getting him to stop."

THIRTY-FOUR

Wade leaned against the post holding up the awning of the shop across the street from The Lucky Lady. His lean frame seemed every bit as tough and unyielding as the lumber supporting him and as the winds rolled by, they barely caused him to stir.

There were others standing nearby, but none of them seemed as intense and unmoving as Wade. The man with the brushy mustache was every bit the calm within the storm as the few Enforcers he'd selected to come with him that day shifted back and forth on their feet or even started pacing along the boardwalk.

But Wade didn't move. His eyes were fixed upon The Lady so hard that they barely took a moment to blink. Every so often his jaw would clench or his nostrils would flare as he pulled in the occasional breath. Besides that, however, he might as well have been just another post that had been sunk into the ground.

Lowell wasn't with them. He was back at Dutch's compound on the outskirts of town nursing the wounds that had been given to him not only during the previous night's fight, but the ones he'd gotten from Dutch himself. That wasn't exactly Lowell's decision, however. Wade

had been the one to keep him behind and he wasn't about
to hear another word about it.

Most of the uncomfortable shifting and pacing from
the Enforcers was due to Lowell's absence. When they
knew they couldn't say anything without risking being put
in a sick bed right next to Lowell himself, their anxious-
ness only grew.

"Stand still," Wade snarled to the closest Enforcer to
him. "I swear you're all pacing around like a bunch'a
goddamn kids."

Although there was still plenty of uneasiness to go
around, every one of the Enforcers stood so still that it
seemed their feet had suddenly dug roots into the ground.
Wade knew what their problem was. He even knew how to
fix it. The only reason he'd been waiting was that he also
knew better than to charge into a fight when he was angry.

Only men that didn't know any better fought like that.

Men who fought while angry had a bad habit of getting
their asses beat or their brains blown out the back of their
skulls.

Unable to contain himself any longer, the closest Enforcer to Wade took a half-step forward and said, "Dutch
wanted us to do something about what happened in there,
Wade."

"Yeah."

The other man glanced between Wade and The Lucky
Lady as though he didn't know which of them was going
to move first. "Then, shouldn't we do what we were
told?"

When Wade's head slowly turned to look at the other
man full-on, his eyes were burning with such intensity
that they practically flickered in their sockets. "You think
I didn't hear what Dutch said?" he asked in a slow, grav-
elly snarl.

"No. It's just that we've been standing out here for—"

"You think I'm deaf?"

"No, Wade. Hell, no, I don't think you're deaf. All I'm saying is—"

"What?" Wade cut in, pulling himself away from the post and taking a quick step toward the Enforcer. "What are you saying? Why don't you make it good and clear for me because I must be stupid as well as deaf. Is that what you're trying to say?"

For every step forward taken by Wade, the man he spoke to took one back. The Enforcer's hands came up and quickly darted away from his gun. Instead, he held the palms out as though he was trying to catch Wade before being overrun. The sight was something similar to a man trying to hold a grizzly at bay with kind words.

"I didn't mean any of that, Wade. Honest. I'm just making sure we do what we're supposed to be doing."

"Don't you worry about that. You hear me?"

"Yeah, yeah. I hear you."

Pulling in a breath through his nose, Wade looked around at the others. "What about the rest of you? Anyone else feel like asking me how I conduct my business?"

Every one of the men had things they wanted to say or questions they wanted to ask. Not one of them, however, said a word.

"Good," Wade said. "I know what we're supposed to do and I ain't been standing out here all day for my health." His eyes flicked over toward the front door of The Lucky Lady and a smirk crept onto his face. "You want to know why we're here? Well, just take a look for yourself."

The Enforcers turned to look as one. And as one, their eyes fell upon a group of figures that came walking out through the main doors.

Leveling a gnarled finger toward the group of well-dressed committee members leaving the saloon, Wade said, "Get 'em."

THIRTY-FIVE

"Now that we know your problem," Clint said, adding, "And you do have a problem. What do you think should be done about it?"

Clint had plenty of his own ideas, but he was interested to know what Victoria had to say. After all, she not only seemed to have a hell of a head on her shoulders, but she had also spent a lot more time around Dutch and his men.

"That was what I wanted to talk to you about," she said. "I've been thinking about this all morning."

"It looked to me that you were in the meeting with those businessmen all morning."

"It feels like longer than that, but you're right. It didn't take long to realize they already had their minds set on what they wanted to do, so I just let them talk to Red while I tried to come up with something better. Unfortunately, I doubt those old men will want to do anything unless they thought of it."

"I'll bet you know ways around that," Clint said, thinking about how she must have been handling Red all this time.

She gave him a look that told Clint she knew what he was referring to and was thinking along those same lines.

"There's not enough time for that," she said. "Knowing these gentlemen, they very well could have contacted this Ironhorse person already."

"Could be."

"That's why I've got something else in mind altogether."

At that moment, Clint could detect something else going on beneath her surface. It would have been easy for someone to miss since the sparkle in her eye blended in perfectly with the seductive quality that was always there anyhow. Clint may not have been immune to that quality himself, but he caught that other certain something all the same.

"I'm not sure if you're going to like this," she warned.

"Try me."

A few minutes later, the door to Victoria's office slammed open and Clint came stomping out. The look on his face was enough for anyone to see that he'd already been pushed to his limit and something he'd just heard had pushed him just a few inches over it.

Clint wasn't exactly running out of the office, but the grim expression on his face and the power in his stride was good enough to clear a path for him through the customers gathered at or near the bar. The door to the office swung shut, but didn't make it all the way closed before it was pulled open again.

"Clint," Victoria said as she stepped into the doorway and held it open. "Wait. Please!"

But Clint wasn't listening to her. It seemed that the only thing in that room of which he was aware was the space a few feet in front of him as he stormed toward the casino. Several of Red's brawlers watched the exchange and started to step in to flag Clint down simply because Victoria seemed desperate to get him back.

One glance from Clint directly at them was like a hot

poker being shoved in their faces and the brawlers immediately backed off.

Still standing in the doorway, Victoria started to rush after him, but stopped after only making it a few feet. She knew that chasing after him would have gotten her nowhere and very well might have pushed Clint out of The Lucky Lady for good.

But Victoria hadn't gotten as far as she had in life without seeing more than one angle. She knew chasing after him wasn't her only option, just as she knew that she had to pick the second best option before her time ran out.

Swinging back around to face her office, she found Solomon already standing behind her, filling up most of the doorway. "Well, go after him," she shouted to the hulking figure. "Bring him back, so we can finish what we were talking about."

Solomon took a step out of the doorway so he could straighten up to his full height. "You want me to bring him back whether he wants to come or not?"

The big man didn't need to try and put an ominous tone in his voice to let Victoria know what he was asking. His words alone sounded ominous enough on their own.

She thought about it for a second and shook her head. "No, just try to convince him to come with you. If he doesn't want to, just let him go and I can try later."

"Yes, ma'am." With that, Solomon strode past the bar to follow in Clint's tracks. He didn't have to walk quickly to close the space between them since his strides were already large enough to do that in no time at all.

Victoria stood and watched her bodyguard go after Clint and didn't take her eyes off of him until Solomon was in the next room. Only then did she notice all the other customers and workers taking in the scene as though they'd just watched a small performance.

Frustrated, Victoria let out a breath and spoke to everyone around her. "Well, what are you all looking at? Just go back to your drinks and mind your business."

Stepping back into her office, Victoria shut her door and headed straight for the glass of wine that was waiting for her on the little round table near the wall. She picked up the glass and took a slow sip that allowed some of the wine to linger for a few moments against her lips. The touch of the wine was relaxing and it slowed the pounding of her heart to a manageable thump.

Just as she was about to take another sip, there was a knocking on the door that was way too timid for it to be Solomon.

"Yes?" she said. "What is it?"

The door came open an inch or so and the barkeep stuck his nose inside. "Umm, Miss Lauren? Something's happened."

"What?" she asked, expecting to hear about something regarding Clint or Solomon.

"It's Red. Him and the rest of the committee were taken by the Enforcers."

Victoria's eyes widened and the wineglass slipped from her fingers.

THIRTY-SIX

"Hello there, Red. I bet you weren't expecting to see me today."

Red blinked away some of the cobwebs that had gathered inside his skull. The pain was from getting knocked on the temple mixed with the pain in his arms and wrists from being held and dragged all the way from The Lady like some calf in a rodeo.

He looked around the room and recognized it immediately. He also recognized the faces of the other committee members propped up in their own chairs against the wall. The businessmen appeared to be alive, but none of them were conscious just yet.

Turning his eyes to the man who'd just addressed him, Red said, "I also wasn't expecting you to make a stupid move like this, Dutch. Even you got to know that Marshal Camms won't be able to ignore this like he does all the other shit you pull around here."

Dutch was half leaning and half sitting on the edge of his own desk which was almost the length of a full-sized coffin. "You think I give a shit what that useless excuse for a lawman likes or doesn't like? You think it even matters anymore?"

Red's eyes narrowed and he looked over to the unconscious committee members. "What do you mean it doesn't matter anymore?"

Watching the other man squirm, Dutch smirked and glanced over at the committee members himself. "You think they're gonna wake up and save you, Red? Is that it? You think those old timers are gonna hear what I'm saying so they can help you in some way?"

Leaning in closer toward Red, Dutch grinned in a way that was distinctly wolfish. "You think they're even gonna wake up at all?"

"Oh my God," Red whispered. "You didn't . . ." He let his question trail off as though he was afraid to finish it.

Dutch let the other man dangle for a few moments before allowing himself to laugh and push off of his desk. "Nah, I didn't do anything like that. Not yet anyway. Having you in here dirties up my office enough without some stinkin' corpses laying around. I wanted you all here so you could listen to what I have to say, but since you're the only one awake right now, I'll start there."

"If you wanted to talk to us, all you needed to do was come to the meeting. You were invited to the first one and to all the others since."

"Yeah, but I don't take to discussing business with whores."

Red's eye twitched when he heard that. "Victoria's not a whore," he said in a warning tone.

"Oh, that's right. She's not a whore no more, but she was one when you first met her." Leering at Red, Dutch knew he was getting under the other man's skin. "Tell me, did you at least get to fuck her before she started thinking she was all respectable?"

It wasn't until he heard the chuckling around him that Red even realized there were more people in the room. A quick look around was all it took for him to spot a couple of the Enforcers leaning against the wall behind his chair and those of the committee members.

Despite the firepower that was evident on each of the Enforcers, Red still turned his angry glare toward Dutch. "She's not a whore. She's a good friend of mine and whatever she did in the past, it sure as hell ain't half as bad as what you do now. I'm surprised you can sleep with yourself at night."

"I'm just a businessman and not much different from all you fine gentlemen gathered here."

"Like hell! You're a thug who steals the money that we all earn after an honest day's work. You're not even much of a thug because you got to have all these hired guns do your dirty work for you."

Dutch put on an exaggerated frown. "Aw, you're about to hurt my feelings."

"That ain't even possible for a man without a soul."

"So what am I supposed to do now, Red? You want me to see the error of my ways, repent and open some store so I can break my back working like the rest of you shit heels? Don't make me laugh."

"Then what do you want from us?" Red asked, unable to mask the desperation that was creeping into his voice. "Why bring us all here when you could have just come and talked to us the proper way?"

"Because I didn't just want to talk." Snapping his fingers at one of his men, Dutch said, "Wake them up. All of them. I want them to see this."

The Enforcers stepped away from the wall and stalked toward the committee members that were bound to their chairs. Some of the older men had been faking their unconsciousness, but made sure to snap their eyes open when they felt the heavy footsteps coming their way.

One by one, the rest of the businessmen were woken up by rough smacks to their faces. A few of them were nearly rattled right back into their slumber as their chairs were violently shaken by the Enforcer assigned to them. Soon, all the older men were awake and trying to figure out what had happened after stepping out of The Lucky Lady's front door.

Dutch sat on the edge of his desk with his arms folded across his chest. He watched the men being forced awake with no small amount of amusement. Once the Enforcers were through, Dutch stood back up and cleared his throat as if he meant to call his own meeting to order.

"All right then," Dutch said. "Now that all of you are awake, I'm sure you'd like to know what's going on. First off, I want to tell you that I know all about your little plan to hire someone to come and wipe out me and my boys."

All of the whispers and hushed questions coming from the committee members stopped. The older men froze, a few of whom still had their mouths hanging open with unfinished words.

Nodding slowly while looking at the older men, Dutch let his eyes settle squarely upon Red. "Yeah, that's what I thought. You see, I knew you fellas weren't as cordial as you'd want me to believe. And here I've been trying to work with you to keep your businesses from being damaged by the rough element we all know comes through here."

Although that rough element was standing in that room or close by at that very moment, none of the committee members figured it was a good time to point that out. Something was brewing in that room. Everyone could feel it as though the clouds had rolled in and the wind took on a deathly chill.

"Now, which one of you wants to see me dead?" Dutch asked.

Suddenly, the chill in that room got bad enough to freeze the marrow inside each committee member's bones.

THIRTY-SEVEN

Bo sat at his normal table that was situated between the casino and the bar area. If he wasn't on his feet in The Lucky Lady, he was at that table. In fact, he was such a fixture there that hardly anyone took notice of him anymore and that was just the way he liked it.

From his vantage point, he could watch what went on in both major areas of the saloon, keep tabs on the front door and even watch the dancing girls when they were parading around onstage. He had to strain a bit, but he could also see the door to Victoria's office. He didn't need a special spot to see when Clint came storming out and he would have had to be blind to miss Solomon wherever that giant went.

It had been a few moments since the two men had left, but Victoria still stood by waiting for them to return. Finally, she stepped back inside and shut the door. Even from where he was sitting, Bo could tell that she was most certainly not happy.

Bo twisted around in his chair to face the casino. Now that Solomon was no longer standing, the big man wasn't so easy to spot. The task wasn't entirely difficult either, since the man still had a good couple of inches on the rest of the seated people.

The place was filling up, so it was difficult to see much more than the top of Solomon's head. After standing up to stretch his legs, Bo got a good enough view to see that Clint Adams was, indeed, sitting at that table with Solomon. There seemed to be some tension between those two as well and Bo wasn't about to let it go too long before he found out what the hell was going on.

After all, that was his job.

Clint sat at the table across from the huge man who sat upon a chair that practically groaned beneath his weight. When he'd stormed out of the back office, Clint could feel every eye in the place focused squarely on him. That had tapered off somewhat, but there was still the occasional glance being thrown his way. Those glances didn't last long, since none of the gawkers seemed interested in attracting either of the men's attention.

"Are you sure about this?" Solomon asked.

"Almost, but not quite. I don't think we'll have to wait too long to find out for sure, though."

Both men spoke in subdued tones. Although their words didn't carry too far, the tone in which they spoke was undeniably hostile. It sounded like fierce whispers or even growls, despite the fact that their words didn't reflect a bit of that.

"Keep your eyes open," Clint said. "If I'm right, we should see something pretty soon."

Solomon gritted his teeth as though he'd been angered by something and turned to look around slowly. "And if you're wrong?"

"Then we'll sit here for a little while and go our separate ways."

"I can go along with that. I don't get to sit down very much when I'm working."

Clint had to suppress a smile. "You don't, huh?"

"Nope. I get paid to be seen and feared. It doesn't do much good if I'm not where folks can see me."

"The life of a bodyguard. Sounds pretty boring."

"Compared to what I used to do, it's not so bad. At least I don't get my hands as dirty since I started working for Miss Lauren."

Watching the big man talk, Clint had no trouble believing that Solomon cleaned up when he took that open seat at that poker game. Solomon's face might as well have been set in granite. His eyes flashed at Clint as though he was about to lunge at any second. Clint kept his expression similarly fearsome, but he didn't have the imposing stature that Solomon had been born with.

"How long should we sit here?" Solomon asked in a way that made it look like he'd just told Clint he was going to tear him apart.

"Another couple of minutes at least. If something's going to happen, it'll happen by then."

"And what are we looking for?"

Clint fell silent, warning Solomon with a quick look that it was no longer safe to speak freely. A few seconds later, someone joined them at their table.

"What was that all about?" Bo asked.

Solomon kept his expression and the tone the same, but this time matched his words to them. "It's between us and Miss Lauren, Bo."

Bo took a step back and raised his hands. "Whoa there. Just asking what the commotion was about. I guess I can just wait for the next commotion to come along. What about you, Clint? Anything you'd like to say?"

"Why do you want to know?"

Pausing for a moment, Bo looked surprised but not offended by the sudden change in Clint's demeanor. "Is he keeping you from saying what you want to say?" Bo asked, hooking a thumb toward Solomon.

"No," Clint replied. He took a breath and stood up, fixing an intense glare onto Solomon. "Stay," he said as though he was giving a command to a dog.

The muscles in Solomon's jaw tensed and his hands tightened around the edge of the table. He didn't get up, however, as Clint and Bo walked to another part of the room.

"Victoria asked me to make a move on Red," Clint said once he and Bo were away from prying ears.

Bo nodded and glanced toward the back office. "Doesn't surprise me. What kind of move is she looking for?"

"The kind that puts a man down for good. About six feet down, to be exact."

"That bitch."

"That's why I stormed out. I didn't come here to kill a man, no matter how much she's willing to pay."

Bo's face still reflected anger, but his eyes didn't follow suit. Instead, they shifted back to Clint as he asked, "How much is she offering?"

"One thousand dollars. You ask me, that's nothing compared to what she's got locked away in that office of hers."

"We can't just let this pass."

"I sure as hell can. This is too messy for me."

"What if I make it worth your while to stay? I mean, since you're already here and all."

"I don't know . . ."

Jumping in when Clint paused, Bo said, "Just don't go anywhere just yet. Head up to your room and I'll send you someone to make you feel better. When I've got things worked out with Red, I'll come get you."

"You're going to tell Red?"

"I guess I should. He'll want to know about this."

Clint thought about it for a moment and finally nodded. "All right then. But I'm not staying here long. You get your ducks in a row quick or I might just not be there when you come for me."

"Don't worry," Bo said, unable to hide his excitement. "I won't be long at all."

After a quick handshake, Clint turned and walked toward the stairs leading to the second floor rooms. He got to the top, stopped, crouched down and waited so he could just see the front door of the saloon. He didn't have to wait long before that door opened and Bo hurried outside.

Clint got a sinking feeling as he went back down the stairs and headed for the table where Solomon and the bartender were exchanging hurried words.

THIRTY-EIGHT

"Red's gone," Solomon said. He spoke as though most of his wind had been expended before Clint got there.

"Gone?" Clint asked. "What do you mean gone?"

"Just what I said. He's gone, along with the rest of the committee members. Someone saw them get swept up and taken away."

"Was it Dutch's men?"

"Whoever told the barkeep what happened didn't want to say that for sure, but who else could it be?"

"Does Victoria know?"

Solomon nodded. "The barkeep told her before he told me."

"Did he tell anyone else?"

"No. Miss Lauren told him to tell me and you. Other than that, he was supposed to keep his mouth shut."

Clint's mind raced. The game they'd been playing had suddenly been taken to the next level and he knew he could either roll with the punches or be knocked out. "All right," he said, forcing himself to slow down so he could talk and be understood. "First things first." Rather than explain himself, Clint strode over to the front window and snagged the barkeep as he went.

155

The smaller man started to pull back just out of reflex but was practically taken completely off his feet when Solomon came by and carried him along with Clint. When he was set back down again, the barkeep wasn't inclined to question what was going on.

"Who else did you tell about this?" Clint asked, swinging around to stare directly into the barkeep's eyes.

"Miss Lauren was the first one I could find that was in charge. After that, I was only supposed to talk to you or Solomon."

"And you stuck to that? You didn't tell anyone before you spoke to Victoria?"

The barkeep shook his head vigorously. "Considering who took those men, I wasn't even sure I should tell anyone. Things happen to folks when they step out of line against the wrong people. That tends to make us think twice before saying much of anything."

Clint looked over to Solomon to see if that was indeed the case. The big man read Clint's question and nodded to verify that the barkeep wasn't just blowing smoke.

Turning back to the barkeep, Clint's mind was once again charging full steam ahead. "Good. Try to keep this one under your hat for as long as you can. How long ago was this?"

"Not long. Wade and the Enforcers were standing around outside for the better part of the day, but there's not much new about that. They got the committee members when they came out and Red was with them."

"Did many others see it?"

The barkeep shook his head. "When Wade and the rest stand around outside the place, they do it to keep people away. It's not the busy time yet so there weren't many other folks about. The only other man who would know about this is Bo. He makes it his business to know these things."

Clint nodded. "You did good. Thanks for coming to us."

Obviously relieved, the barkeep asked, "What should I do now?"

"Just carry on with your work and if anyone asks, just don't say anything. We'll take care of this from here."

The barkeep was more than happy to get back to his post and Solomon stepped up to stand beside Clint who had yet to take his eyes from the window for more than a second or two. Solomon looked out as well.

"You think it's him?" the big man asked.

Clint nodded. "I hate to say it, but yeah. Bo's been sitting at that table of his all day, watching everything that goes on around here. There's no way he would miss something like Red and those others getting swept away by Wade and his boys."

"Did he mention anything about it when he talked to you?" Solomon asked.

"Nope. Not a word. In fact, he said he was going to talk to Red about my little predicament. As for that, he took the news about Victoria's offer pretty well. He blew some smoke my way, but he wasn't too upset about the prospect of losing Red."

"Maybe he just doesn't know about what happened to Red."

"That wouldn't explain why he left the place as soon as he thought I was gone instead of heading to Red's office or anywhere else Red should be right about now. No, he knew Red was gone."

"So Miss Lauren was right?"

"Looks like it. She said there was a spy in here working for Dutch and I think we flushed him out. Now we've got to follow up before they get too full of themselves."

THIRTY-NINE

It had been going on for almost an hour.

In that time, Dutch had gone from speaking in a calm tone of voice to launching into rants and raving about everything that had been going on in Crystall for the last few weeks. Of course, the more he talked, the less sense he made since everything came out with him as the victim and the men tied to their chairs as the heartless bullies.

"I know you wanted to have me killed," Dutch said, addressing all of the committee at once. "Now all I want to know is which one of you thought of it first."

"We told you," Red said, doing his level best to keep his voice from cracking under the strain. "We don't want to have you killed. The money you take from us is breaking our backs, though. We work hard for that money and still we can barely make ends meet."

Dutch was standing in front of one of the older men, glaring at him as though the fellow in the suit was the world's greatest evil. "You think I'm stupid?" Dutch asked, first to Red and then to the man closer to him. "What about you? Do I look stupid to you?"

The only thing that had kept the businessmen from spouting out everything they'd planned was the fact that they all knew they would be killed a couple seconds after their confession. That much was obvious just by watching the deterioration of Dutch's manner from sane to stark raving mad in less than an hour.

"I . . . I . . . I don't . . . I never" was all the older man could get out before Dutch's fist slammed into his face and knocked him back into unconsciousness.

Without saying a word, Dutch drew his pistol and jammed the end of the barrel into the leg of the committee member he'd just knocked out. Without so much as a blink, Dutch pulled his trigger.

The muffled shot sounded more like a thump, followed by the rattle of the older man's chair knocking against the floor as he thrashed in pain. The wound looked like a gaping black pit when Dutch took his gun away. Smoke curled out of the blood-spattered barrel and the old man looked at the gun as though he was staring into the single eye of a monster from his nightmares.

"I've got five more shots in this gun," Red stated, "and I've got plenty more ammunition in my desk. Unlike you fellows, I don't plan on killing anyone here today. But I can spread a whole lot of misery if someone doesn't tell me what I want to know.

"There's someone coming for me, I know that much. That someone has been contracted by someone here in this room. I want to know who decided to go against me, who was hired to do the job and when they're expected to arrive. I know it wasn't Clint Adams because if that was the case I would have seen him by now."

Dutch looked around at each of the terrified faces. As he searched each set of eyes, he brought his gun slowly down to take aim at the men's belt level. From there, he moved the gun a little lower until it was pointed at another committee member's groin.

"Better talk quickly," Dutch said to the man in his sights. "I know you're too old to get that thing of yours to work, but I bet you still want to keep it attached."

The old man was either too tough or too scared to talk. With all the color long since drained from his face, it was hard to tell which of those two options applied to him. Whether out of fear or stubbornness, his lips remained as still as if they'd been painted onto his face. His chest rose and fell at a quickening pace until it got to the point that his breaths were becoming too shallow and too fast.

Not only did Dutch notice this change, but he sunk his teeth into it and did his best to make it worse. If the old man had a wound, Dutch would have jammed his fingers into it and ripped it open wider. As it was, he stalked forward, slowly cocked the hammer back and took his time aiming the pistol between the old man's legs.

Dutch's finger nearly twitched on the trigger when the door to his office was thrown open and someone came rushing inside. The man who entered did so with a full escort of Enforcers, but didn't seem hindered by any one of the armed men.

"Something big's happening," Bo said as he charged inside. "It's got to do with Adams and Miss Lauren."

Regaining his control after almost slipping on the trigger, Dutch kept his gun aimed on target while shifting his eyes toward Bo. "What the hell are you talking about? What happened?"

"They're fixing to kill Red. Miss Lauren tried to get Adams to do it for her, but he got fired up and walked out on her. I think he's ready to be done with them for good."

Dutch's face twisted into a smile. "Is that a fact?" Looking over to Red, he added, "Looks like your perfect little committee has a few holes in it. And here I thought that bitch was just some fancy window dressing."

Going by the look on Red's face, he was too shocked to say much of anything.

"Maybe I don't need to put you fellas through all this

after all," Dutch said. "I mean, if you've already got one of your own gunning for you, what harm would there be in telling me what I want to know?"

Red may have been at a loss for words, but one of the other committee members sure wasn't. The old man sat between the fellow who'd taken the shot to the leg and the one who was about to get shot in the groin. "His name is Nick Ironhorse," the anxious businessman said. "And he's due to arrive any day now."

"What?" Red said, having been snapped out of his stupor.

The old man shrugged and said, "Sorry, Red. We know how close you and Victoria are, but it's all of our livelihoods at stake here. Now, our lives are at risk."

"Now we're getting somewhere," Dutch said. "That answers one of my questions." With that, Dutch placed his gun against the temple of the man who'd just confessed and pulled his trigger.

A crimson mist of blood and pulp was still hanging in the air and dripping off the wall when Dutch turned to the closest Enforcer and said, "I want that bitch dead and I want it to happen now!"

FORTY

Clint didn't hear the gunshot that had taken the life of that committee member. His ears were too full of the slamming sound of his boot meeting the front door of Dutch's storefront and then the slam of that door as it was practically knocked off its hinges. There were only a few men with him since that was all he could round up on such short notice. Solomon was among those men, however, and Clint figured that counted for a lot.

"Where's the men you took?" Clint shouted as he took a step inside the building.

From the outside, the building was just an unmarked storefront that could have been any type of office or place of business. Inside, the first room was just as nondescript, containing not much more than a few coat racks and a couple of chairs scattered about.

Two men were in that room, but they were caught flat-footed and relaxing in those chairs. They'd tried to scramble to their feet, but were unable to get very far before Clint had busted his way inside.

One of the men stopped trying to get off his chair and went for his gun instead. It turned out that was an even worse decision because Clint's hand blazed toward the

Colt at his side and drew the weapon before the other man's trigger was halfway pulled. The Colt barked once and sent a round through the air.

Sparks flew from the Enforcer's weapon and he dropped the pistol as Clint's bullet ripped a crease through his hand. The pain was enough to make his whole body react and that was more than enough to pitch him over backward, toppling him to the floor and taking the chair right along with him.

That left the other man in the room who was looking at the rest of the men who'd come inside with Clint. The Enforcer didn't even see Red's brawlers since all of his attention was focused on the mountain of muscle that was currently lumbering straight toward him.

Solomon reached out with both hands as he raced forward. Moving quicker than what someone might expect from a man of his size, Solomon got to the Enforcer and took hold of the other man the way he might pick up a puppy that had gotten loose. One hand closed around the Enforcer's arm while the other got hold of the seat of his pants. From there, all Solomon had to do was lift and the other man was completely off his feet.

Not quite knowing how to react, the Enforcer kicked and thrashed while letting out a surprised yelp. Before he knew which way was up, he was being flung through the air like a rag doll. His back slammed against the wall and the back of his head was next to follow. After that, everything went black. He didn't even feel it as he was let go and allowed to drop in a heap on the floor.

Clint rushed forward and kicked the gun away before the man he'd shot got a chance to pick it up with his good hand. The moment he sent the dropped pistol skidding to a distant corner, Clint sent his left fist into the other man's gut, doubling him over and taking away what little fight remained in him.

One of the doors leading out of the room came open.

Clint's eyes turned in that direction and he was just able to catch a glimpse of a pair of men standing there, looking back at him over the barrels of their guns. One man knelt in front of the other, forming a classic firing line so both of them could open fire at once.

Clint's reflexes kicked in, but were interrupted by the sound of a roaring voice combined with the thunder of approaching footsteps.

"Watch it, Clint!" Solomon roared as he stampeded toward Clint's position.

The giant threw himself forward while extending his arms. Both massive hands reached Clint easily and were able to bat him aside before the rest of him touched the floor again. Solomon threw himself one way and shoved Clint in the other, clearing the space that was suddenly filled by hot lead as both Enforcers in the doorway pulled their triggers.

As the bullets plowed through the space where Clint had just been standing, he quickly adjusted his aim and fired a shot toward the doorway. The shot was too rushed and the Enforcers had been too prepared, however, and the Colt's round buried itself into the frame.

Even though he hadn't hit anything but wood, Clint still managed to get both of the other men to pull back and wait before they fired again. Looking over to Solomon, Clint gave a quick wave of thanks before scrambling back onto his feet.

Another body filled the doorway and Clint nearly took a shot at it before he noticed that Red was the man standing there. Once again, Clint's reflexes saved a life and he loosened his trigger finger before the Colt's hammer dropped.

"We're coming out," Red said as he threw his hands in the air and his face went pale. "Don't shoot, boys."

"What about the rest?" Clint asked, making sure he could be heard by anyone in the next room. "Send them out or we'll be coming in to get them. And if I hear one more shot, we'll clear out this whole place and figure it was self-defense."

There was a few tense moments when Clint thought he'd made the wrong decision in giving Dutch and his men a chance. Red moved forward slowly at first, but got going quick enough once he was far enough away from his captors. A few moments later, the rest of the committee members came staggering through the door.

All of the businessmen except for one, that is.

Clint was in too big of a hurry to wait around much longer once it was clear that everyone who was able to come out had done so. Besides, he hadn't gotten a precise number of how many members the committee had before he went in. Clint didn't like working without figuring all the angles, but time had been a factor that hadn't left him with much choice.

"Get them out of here," Clint said to Solomon.

"What about you?"

"I'll be right behind you."

Red and the other businessmen were escorted out by Solomon and the brawlers from The Lucky Lady. Clint kept his Colt drawn and his eyes open as he stepped carefully toward the front door. Nobody made a move against him just then, but Clint knew this wasn't the end.

Nothing was ever that easy.

FORTY-ONE

It had been one hell of a day. As a matter of fact, it had been one hell of a couple of days.

Once Clint, Solomon and Red's brawlers got Red and the committee out of Dutch's office, they'd all hunkered down in the hotel rooms of The Lucky Lady. Business had dropped off considerably since nobody else in town needed to be told what was going on between the feuding factions. Even with that in mind, some of the most loyal customers kept themselves parked in their regular seats. To them, this was one hell of a show.

The doctor took up in one of the rooms as well since there were more patients to treat in the saloon than there were in his own office. Most of his time was spent with the man who'd been shot below the belt. That one's screams could be heard for hours and only faded when he passed out from the pain and loss of blood.

Early the next morning, the doctor came out of that room, wiping the sweat from his brow and the blood from his hands.

"How is he?" Clint asked.

The doctor shook his head. "He's gone. Actually, I'm surprised he made it this long. There wasn't much we could do since he lost a good deal of blood before I got to him. He wasn't a young man and he really didn't have much chance of fighting through all that pain and shock."

Clint nodded grimly. "So that makes two."

"Red told you about the one that was killed?"

"Yeah."

"Are you going to pay Marshal Camms a visit?"

"If he hasn't done anything by now, he's not going to do anything at all. He's either on Dutch's payroll or too scared to get involved. Either way, he's useless."

"True enough."

Clint took a moment to truly look at the doctor. The man wasn't too far into his forties, but the wear on his face made him look at least two decades older. "Why don't you get some rest, doc? Aren't bruises and bumps pretty much the extent of the injuries that're left?"

"There's a few flesh wounds, but they just need some fresh dressings. Once I—"

"You go get your rest," Victoria cut in as she stepped out of one of the nearby rooms. "I'll change those dressings and check in on the others." When she saw the doctor start to protest, she held up her hand and said, "I insist."

"All right then," the doctor finally conceded. "But I'll be back in an hour or so to make my rounds."

"Sounds good."

Clint gave the doctor a comforting pat on the back and felt the other man almost fall over from that little bit of contact. He was certain the physician was asleep the moment he got into his room. Now that they were alone in the hall, Clint looked over to Victoria and motioned for her to walk with him.

"What time is it?" he asked as he reached for his pocket watch.

"Almost five thirty. Clint, you could use some rest yourself."

"Jesus. I didn't realize it was that late."

"Did you hear what I said? You need to rest."

"Not while this is still going on," Clint replied. "Everyone has sat back for too long already and let Dutch walk where he wants and do what he pleases. That's got to end."

"But I didn't want you to get involved like this. You're not a hired gun and I already feel so bad for dragging you into this mess."

Clint stopped walking and turned to look at her directly. Reaching out, he put his hands on Victoria's shoulders and rubbed along the length of her arms. He could feel the tension that was there and could also feel some of that tension melt away beneath his soothing touch.

"I know I don't have to be here," Clint said. "Neither do you. Why shouldn't you just pick up and leave? You know you could start another saloon somewhere else that's just as good, if not better, than The Lady."

"I know." Victoria lowered her eyes and paused for a moment. When she looked back up again, there was something else in her expression that had always been there, but usually was kept further beneath the surface. It was a steely resolve that made her look more formidable than Clint had seen her.

"But there's no reason for me to move," she said. "I'm not the one doing anything wrong. Dutch is and he's been wronging this whole town for way too long."

Clint nodded, keeping his hands on her sides and holding her firmly. "That's why I'm staying too. If there's something a man can do to help when others are getting walked over, then there's no excuse for holding back. Now that Dutch has taken things to the next level, I don't have any option but to stay. I'm not about to ride off and let him get away with murder."

"But you may get hurt too, Clint. And don't forget that Ironhorse is coming. What happens when—"

"First we deal with Dutch," Clint interrupted. "Then we'll deal with Ironhorse."

Nodding, Victoria said, "All right." With that, she lowered her head so she could rest it against Clint's chest and allowed herself to be pulled in closer to him.

She melted into Clint's arms and he could feel her spirits rising when he embraced her tightly. For a few seconds, they just stood there in the hall, letting the rest of the world go by for a while. He didn't forget about what needed to be done, but Clint took those moments to draw some strength from Victoria and to give her some of his as well.

"When are you going back over there?" Victoria asked in a quiet, almost hesitant voice.

"Soon."

"What can I do to help?"

"Take the boys you've got working security and make sure they're ready for anything. I'll only need to take one or two of them with me."

"Won't you need more than that?"

"No," Clint replied. "Any more than that would just get in my way."

FORTY-TWO

Wade paced the same stretch of floor that he'd been walking for the last hour. Before that, he'd been content to get his Enforcers up to snuff and make sure they were ready when the order came to clean out that fucking saloon once and for all. But that order hadn't come yet, which got Wade in a worse mood with every passing hour.

His men were ready and they needed to move fast. Before now, Dutch was the type to do his damage and let the old men stew before hitting them again. That was a fine tactic for the past. Things have changed and there was no longer just a bunch of old men and inexperienced bar fighters to deal with.

They had bigger problems now and there was plenty more lined up behind Clint Adams.

Wade came to a stop and listened to see if he could still hear the voices coming from the biggest room on the second floor of the building. Just when he thought he could finally hear some quiet, those voices came back and Wade knew Dutch was still too busy to talk. Shaking his head, Wade wondered if he should just cut his losses and let Dutch handle himself for a change. After all, if he didn't seem to care about possibly losing everything they'd built, why should Wade be worried? Plenty of money had been made and now was just as good a time to leave as any.

But then Wade felt that pang in his gut that simply wouldn't let him think like that. He was the man to put fear into others, not be driven away. He was the man who took what he wanted, not the one who stored away what he could so he could finally sneak away like a kid running away from home.

Wade had invested a lot into the town of Crystall and if Dutch wanted to piss it away, Wade would be the man to step in and take it from him. All he needed to do was get through this batch of trouble and the Enforcers would be behind him when Wade made his move for the top.

Thinking ahead that far made Wade even more anxious. He couldn't just wait for Dutch to have his fun. There were things to do and if they didn't get done, then the whole house of cards would come tumbling down.

"Dutch!" Wade shouted to the door as he pounded his fist against the wood. "Come on out of there, for Christ's sake!"

Dutch had picked her because of her looks. It wasn't just because the girl was pretty. It wasn't just because she was young. It was because she had the beautiful face, sparkling eyes and golden hair that reminded him of another woman he knew he could never possess.

Despite all of his success, Dutch knew he would never be able to get his hands on Victoria Lauren unless he took her by force. And though he wasn't completely against such a thing, there was a part of him that also knew she had enough fire in her to fight him off until one of them was either badly hurt or even dead.

"You bitch," he snarled as he grabbed hold of the blond girl he'd paid to be his own exclusive lover. "You fucking bitch."

The blonde had been concerned when he would talk like this when they were having sex at first, but soon learned that it was just the way he wanted it. He came close to hitting her several times, but couldn't quite seem to bring himself to do it. She didn't know why and didn't care. She was paid well and only had to provide her services on those rare occasions when he could stay hard long enough to enter her.

This was one of those times. In fact, he was so hard and so intense that Dutch was actually fucking her hard enough for the girl to get some pleasure out of it.

Grabbing hold of her hips, Dutch knelt between her open legs and thrust into her as hard as he could. He looked down at her naked breasts and erect nipples, thinking that Victoria's body couldn't be much different. After what he'd done to Red and his men, Dutch knew that Victoria got a good, long look at the power she was up against. And he liked to think that when she saw just how strong Dutch truly was, she got just as wet as the girl spread out in front of him.

Dutch pumped in and out of her, picturing how Victoria's face would clench and how her voice would sound when she moaned like the blonde on his bed. The girl's skin was smooth and even the soft hair between her legs was like fine, gold down.

The lips of her pussy were light pink and open wide. She slipped her fingers between her legs to spread herself open a little more and also to gently rub her clitoris.

"You like that, whore?" Dutch grunted.

"Yeah," the girl replied with a little more feeling than usual. "Oh yeah, just like that. Nice and hard."

Dutch loved it when she told him what to do. Victoria was always giving orders and he knew that wasn't just when it came to business. Grabbing onto the girl's hips a little tighter, Dutch put all of his strength behind his thrusts and leaned his head back to revel in the moment.

Beneath him, the girl pumped her hips up and down. She matched his rhythm perfectly until she thought that she might actually be allowed to climax this time as well. His thrusts sped up and his hold on her tightened.

"You little bitch," he snarled as he rushed toward orgasm. "You sweet little whore."

Dutch exploded inside of her and was left light-headed. He pushed into her a few more times before pulling out and climbing down from the bed. He could hear the knocking as well as Wade's voice coming from the other side of the door. Dutch knew the other man would be angry, but it was tradition to pay the blonde a visit after a particularly good night. And with the committee's blood still on his floor, it had been an extremely good couple of nights.

"Hold on!" Dutch shouted as he went to his neat stack of clothes and put them back on. Looking over to the blonde, he asked, "Was that good?"

She nodded. "The best ever."

Leaving a wad of bills on the dresser, Dutch strapped on his gun belt and left.

The blonde slid under the covers and slipped her hand between her legs. She began to massage her moist pussy and make vigorous circles over her still-sensitive clitoris. Sometimes, if a girl wanted it done right she had to do it herself.

FORTY-THREE

"This ain't the time to celebrate," Wade said as he walked beside Dutch. "Not with Adams still out there and especially now that he knows about Bo."

"Who knows about Bo?"

Wade had to fight back the frustration he felt at having to explain everything to a man who should have been smart enough to figure it out on his own. "He put that cock and bull story out there to see who would bite and Bo sank his teeth right in."

"Are you sure about that?"

"It's what I would have done to smoke out a spy. Victoria's had her suspicions for a while, but you never listen to me when I tell you that something's wrong. Now she wants to kill Red? That's goddamn ridiculous."

Dutch stopped just short of walking into his office and glared at Wade. "Well, excuse the hell out of me if we're not all as smart as you. There's plenty I got to tend to and still everything's going along just fine."

"Things to tend to?" Wade asked sarcastically. "Like what? Fucking that kept whore instead of dealing with Clint Adams knocking on your door? And if everything's going so fine, how come we still got Ironhorse to tend to?

He's no joke, Dutch, and you may just find that out when he rolls through here and burns this place to the ground."

"You want to see flames? You want to see me take care of things? Fine! I want you to set a torch to The Lucky Lady and every other business owned by someone in that goddamn committee."

Wade took a step back from the other man the moment he saw the crazy spark in Dutch's eyes.

"You heard me! Torch it all! What's the matter? You chicken shit now that it's time to move?"

"You don't want to do this, Dutch. What's the use of controlling something that you're just going to burn down? You've got to think about what you're—"

"Oh I've thought about it plenty," Dutch interrupted. "Now's the time for you to earn your salary, shut your mouth and do what I say. Are you gonna do that or not?"

Dutch waited for a few pounding heartbeats. When he saw that Wade wasn't about to jump at the commands he'd been given, Dutch flung open his office door and shouted for someone who would.

"Lowell! Get your ass in here!"

It took a little bit, but Lowell answered Dutch's call. His face was swollen to twice its size and his jaw was covered with a dark, purple bruise. His mouth was stuck partially open, but at least he was no longer walking funny from the kick he'd taken south of his border.

"Yeah," was all Lowell said as he stepped into the room.

Dutch turned to Lowell as though he was looking at his favorite son. "I want to solve our problems with Red and his blond whore once and for all and I want you to do it me. It seems that Wade here has lost his taste for the rough work."

Wade rolled his eyes in response to Lowell's questioning gaze.

Strutting around like a newly crowned prince, Dutch

continued. "Gather up all the Enforcers and put a torch to the shops and businesses owned by every member of that committee that's been a thorn in our sides. Understand?"

Lowell nodded.

"Start with some of the smaller places and work up to The Lucky Lady. But don't save her for last. I want to see that shit hole burning within the hour. Think you can do that?"

"Yeah, but—"

Dutch stopped him with a waggling finger in Lowell's face. "Can you handle this on your own or not?"

Before Lowell could answer, Wade stepped up to his side. "If this is gotta be done, he won't be on his own."

Dutch regarded Wade for a moment before nodding and slapping the other man on the back. "I knew you'd come around, Wade. You know which plays to back. But I'm still giving Lowell the reins on this one."

"Sure," Wade said. "Let's just get this over with."

"Don't let me keep you." With that, Dutch strutted past his desk and stood at the window overlooking the bulk of town. He rocked back and forth on his heels, smiling broadly as though he could already see the smoke billowing from certain windows.

Wade and Lowell headed downstairs. The rest of the Enforcers had heard the commotion and were ready to join them as they stomped outside and poured into the street. A few of the more eager gunmen were already clutching torches.

FORTY-FOUR

Wade's expression became more and more grim the farther he got from Dutch's office. By the time he was outside, he looked ready to put his fist through the first wall he could reach. Cocking his head to one side, he shot a look toward the closest Enforcer that could have melted steel.

"Put those goddamn torches out," Wade ordered.

Lowell was beside him at first, but had fallen behind when Wade picked up his pace. "But Dutch said to—"

"I don't give a rat's ass what Dutch said. We conduct our business and some of that means we need to roll over a few people, but I didn't sign on to burn down half this town." Looking at each Enforcer in turn, he asked, "What about you men?"

None of the gunmen were going to fight him on the matter, but a few of them didn't look too happy about the decision either. To them, Wade said, "We'll torch The Lady, but that's all. I think this whole town's had their fill of that place anyhow. Does that sit well with the rest of you?"

Now, everyone in the group was happy and all but two of the torch bearers put out their flames. Those two torches that remained lit only stayed that way until the group approached the next corner and was about to make the turn. Two shots blasted through the air, one for each torch, clipping off the burning tips and sending them into the dirt.

"I knew all I had to do was wait," Clint said as he stepped into the street in front of the group. "It was only a matter of time before the rats all came scurrying out of their hole."

"Step aside, Adams," Wade snarled. "This matter don't concern you."

"It does now."

"Why? Because Red's paying you? We'll match it and then some."

"You know that's not it," Clint replied. "You and your boss have stepped way over the line and this has got to stop. Since I have yet to see the law in this town, that duty falls to whoever's man enough to accept it."

"And that'd be you, I take it?"

"For starters."

Clint's last words were punctuated by the sound of heavy footsteps pounding against wooden planks as Solomon emerged from the alley to the left of the Enforcers. The big man seemed to fill every bit of space between the two buildings and the shotgun he carried seemed like a toy in his massive hands.

The Enforcers tensed at the same time. The shift could be felt in the air like a tremor running below everyone's feet. Wade could feel it too. And though he wanted to stop anything before it started, the rest of the men were already too tightly wound up to be diverted so easily.

"We don't want to—" was all Wade managed to get out before the first of the Enforcers went for his gun.

Solomon already had his shotgun pointed at the group and all it took was a simple shift to get the barrel aimed at the man who'd made the first move. The shotgun's roar combined with the crack of pistol fire as both men fired simultaneously. Lead filled the air and it was only a simple matter of numbers to figure who would score the hit.

The Enforcer got one bullet to fly while Solomon let loose an entire load of buckshot. The big man's target caught most of it and went down as the front of his chest was ripped open. But with so many men standing together, the ones on either side of Solomon's target caught some lead as well, which spurred them to action.

Clint waited until he got a good line on one of the men who posed a genuine threat. From his vantage in the street, he could see the front of the group better than Solomon could. That was how he managed to see Lowell drawing his pistol before Solomon could react to it.

Lowell almost cleared leather before Clint drew, took quick aim and pulled his trigger. The Colt barked once, sending a shot straight into Lowell's chest. The impact staggered him back a few steps, but didn't put him down. Apparently, the beatings he'd taken had toughened him up because he turned his gaze as well as his weapon in Clint's direction.

With the Colt already on target, all that remained for Clint to do was think about taking the shot and he once again felt the modified pistol buck against his palm. In the blink of an eye, Lowell's head was snapping back and his arms were dropping uselessly at his sides. As his head lolled forward like a doll's, Lowell dropped to one knee before falling face-first into the dust.

Solomon strode directly toward the group of Enforcers, wielding his shotgun like a club rather than taking another shot at the entire group. The scattergun may have been indiscriminate when fired, but it became a precision weapon when Solomon gripped it by the barrel and swung it at one man at a time.

There was a hiss from the barrel against Solomon's hands since it had just been fired, but the big man hardly seemed to notice. Instead, he gritted his teeth against the burning and used it to put some extra fuel behind his swings. The first one caught one of the Enforcers squarely on the side of the head, knocking the man out and dropping him like a sack of rocks.

The next swing caused the entire group to break up in all directions, but Solomon managed to clip one of them on the shoulder with the shotgun's handle. That spun the man around on his toes and when the Enforcer started to bring his gun up, Solomon took hold of that hand and used it to yank him practically out of his boots. With a mighty heave, Solomon tossed the Enforcer and cracked him on the back of the head with his makeshift club. Letting him go at just the right moment, Solomon dumped the Enforcer on top of Lowell's body, making the start of a beefy pile.

Clint saw that Solomon had the bulk of the group well in hand, so he went straight for the head of the Enforcers. So far, Wade seemed to be staying out of the fight, but Clint knew that if Wade changed his mind that could spell deadly trouble for him as well as Solomon.

As if sensing that Clint was coming up to him, Wade spun around and brought up his pistol, and almost as quickly lifted his Colt. For a moment, both men just stared at each other.

"You can end this now," Clint said as Solomon flipped his shotgun around to point the business end at the few Enforcers that were still on their feet.

Wade surprised the hell out of Clint by nodding and letting his gun drop from his fingers. "Coming from any other man, I might expect a bullet in the back. But from what I've heard about you, Adams, I think I can take you up on that deal."

Clint always tried to give a man a way out before sending him to his grave. After having that offer spat back at him so many times, he almost didn't know what to do when someone actually used their head as something else except for a bull's-eye.

"What about Dutch?" Clint asked.

"I can leave it up to you. Or," Wade added, nodding toward the sides of the street, "I could leave it up to them."

Clint looked quickly and saw that Red, Victoria as well as most of the old men he'd saved from Dutch's place were gathered to watch the fight. There were others there as well, but they didn't have quite as much at stake so they seemed more intent on keeping their heads down.

Suddenly, Wade's eyes locked on something a little farther away and he let out a grumbling breath. "Aww, hell. Looks like we're too late to worry about any of this."

Keeping his gun trained on Wade, Clint moved himself as well as the other man around so he could get a look at what Wade was talking about. He spotted the other group of men immediately and even across the distance that separated them, there was no mistaking the gnarled face of Nick Ironhorse.

FORTY-FIVE

Ironhorse wasn't a tall man. He wasn't even a particularly big man. In fact, on first glance, he appeared to be lanky and on the short side. But that all changed once that same observer looked at the man's face. Covered with scars and tanned to a leathery brown, Ironhorse looked as though he'd walked from one end of a desert to another without sipping a drop.

His eyes were weathered slits with nothing but black showing through from the pupils. His lips curled into a sneer to give a glimpse of chipped teeth. There were only three men with him, but that seemed to be more than enough for Ironhorse to roll over yet another town if left unchecked.

Clint stepped forward and could hear Solomon following. Wade stayed right where he was and made sure none of the other Enforcers made any sudden moves.

"Where's Mabry?" Ironhorse snarled.

Assuming that was the name of the committee member who'd contacted Ironhorse, Clint nodded toward the crowd of old men. "He's right there, but he's not the one you need to talk to."

Ironhorse took that as a challenge and his eyes flared

slightly to the occasion. Squaring off with Clint, he asked, "Who're you?"

"Clint Adams."

Ironhorse nodded slightly. "I heard'a you and I ain't afraid'a you."

"That's fine with me on both counts."

"Then what do ya want?"

"I wanted to let you know that you're not going to get a bit of trouble from me."

Although there was only a slight murmur throughout the crowd, Clint could feel the surprise and dread around him as though it was a wave of heat.

"But I also wanted to tell you your contract has been changed," Clint added.

Cocking his head to one side and taking a look around, Ironhorse looked like a hungry dog eyeing a nearby steak. "I didn't come all this way for nothin'."

"Of course you didn't. What I want from you is to keep an eye on that man right there," Clint said, turning and pointing up to the window where a solitary figure looked down on what had been going on at street level. "That's Dutch Wilson. He's the man you were sent after."

Ironhorse's lips curled back slightly and he took a reflexive step toward Dutch's office. He stopped short, however, and looked back to Clint. "What's changed?"

"He's going to leave this town and take all his men with him. Once they're a couple miles away, it doesn't matter where they go just so long as they don't come back here. Your job is to escort them out of here and keep them out."

The single laugh that came from Ironhorse's mouth sounded more like a bull snorting. "I ain't no wet nurse."

"I know that. You came here to do a job for a fee and you'll get that fee." Turning slightly toward the crowd, but without taking his eyes off of Ironhorse, Clint said,

"Pay the man what you agreed to, Mabry. And be quick about it."

With a little encouragement from Victoria, by way of a none-too-gentle shove, Mabry rushed away and came back with a cigar box. It took a few minutes and in that time, the only sound that could be heard was the rustle of the wind and the clatter of a few loose shutters.

Mabry walked toward the street, headed toward Iron-horse, but then made his way to Clint's side instead. He handed the box over, but didn't seem too happy about it.

"I assume it's all here?" Clint asked the trembling old man whom he recognized as one of the people he'd rescued from Dutch's office. When he got a nod in response to his question, Clint stepped forward and handed the box to Ironhorse.

"Take it," Clint said. "They offered it to you, so it's only right that they pay."

After counting the money inside the box, Ironhorse said, "This'll get those fellas an escort out of town, but this ain't enough to drag myself all the way back here again."

"I figured as much. Instead, you can come by to collect your profits from The Lucky Lady saloon. When you check in, they'll have ten percent of the monthly profits to pay you for your services. If you find Dutch or any of his men here, you can do what you came to do in the first place."

Ironhorse's face twisted into a gnarled smile.

"And," Clint added, "if I hear about you trying to take more than your percentage or if you harm anyone or anything else in this town besides Dutch or his men, I will make it my business to track you down and drop you where you stand. Is that clear?"

There was no mistaking the look on Clint's face. Even Ironhorse's black, soulless eyes could see that he meant business.

"Yeah. It's clear," Ironhorse said.

"Then be so kind as to show these men out of town."

The process was short and sweet. All Ironhorse had to do was take two steps toward Dutch's office and Dutch as well as all his Enforcers tossed their guns away and started walking toward their horses. Clint watched, knowing that the other men's fear of this monster that had come into their midst was enough to get them out after being pounded for the last couple days by Clint and Red's brawlers.

"You think they'll come back?" Victoria asked as she stepped up beside Clint.

"Dutch? Hell, no. He's broken. You can see that in his eyes. By the looks of it, I'd say Wade will be more of a threat to him now than anyone else. As for Ironhorse, he knows it's more profitable for him to keep his end of the deal. After all, I will be checking in from time to time to make sure I invested ten out of my twenty-five percent interest wisely as well as to collect my own fifteen percent share of The Lady."

She hugged him and kissed him gently. "I should just take Ironhorse's ten percent out of Red's share."

"Nah, it was my idea so I'll pay for it. Just remember that bringing Ironhorse into this was the committee's idea and if that backfires, they'll have to pay for it too. You should be alright, but—"

She stopped him with another quick kiss. "We'll deal with it, Clint. Thanks for everything. Be sure to check in soon, though. I promise you'll have more waiting for you than just your fifteen percent."

Watch for

THE CANADIAN JOB

276th novel in the exciting GUNSMITH series
from Jove

Coming in December!

J. R. ROBERTS

THE GUNSMITH

J GIANT ACTION! GIANT ADVENTURE!

THE GUNSMITH

GIANT

GIANT WESTERNS FEATURING THE GUNSMITH

TALES FROM THE WHITE ELEPHANT
0-515-13182-2

THE MARSHALL OF KINGDOM
0-515-13417-1

THE GHOST OF BILLY THE KID
0-515-13622-0

LITTLE SURESHOT AND THE WILD WEST SHOW
0-515-13851-7

**AVAILABLE WHEREVER BOOKS ARE SOLD OR AT
WWW.PENGUIN.COM**